THE BEST MAN TO DIE
by Ruth Rendell

The dead man lay face down; someone
had smashed in the back of his head with a
heavy smooth object.

Chief Inspector Wexford watched a thin
pale hand rise slowly, its fingers hanging yet
pointed toward him.

"Christ," a man said softly, "just last
night I was having a drink with him at the
Dragon . . . it's *good old Charlie!*"

"Who killed 'good old Charlie' will keep
you guessing!"
　　　　　　　　　—*Columbus Dispatch*

"A thriller."
　　　　　　　　　—*Publishers Weekly*

"A challenging puzzle . . . the characteriza-
tion is exceptional."
　　　　　　　　　—*San Rafael Journal*

THE BEST MAN TO DIE

RUTH RENDELL

BALLANTINE BOOKS • NEW YORK

*All of the characters in this book
are fictitious, and any resemblance
to actual persons, living or dead,
is purely coincidental.*

Library of Congress Catalog Card Number: 70-97683

ISBN 0-345-29693-1

This edition published by arrangement with
Doubleday & Co., Inc.

Manufactured in the United States of America

First Ballantine Books Edition: March 1975
Second Printing: June 1981

For George and Dora Herbert,
in gratitude for their helpful advice

1

JACK PERTWEE WAS getting married in the morning and the Kingsmarkham and District Darts Club were in the Dragon to give him what George Carter called a send-off.

'I don't like the sound of that, George,' said Jack. 'I'm getting married, not buried.'

'It comes to the same thing.'

'Thanks very much. I'll buy you another drink for that.' He moved up to the bar but the darts club chairman intercepted him.

'My round, Jack. Don't you take any notice of George. Marilyn's a lovely girl and you're a lucky man. I know I speak for us all when I say there's no one here who wouldn't like to be in your shoes tomorrow.'

'His pyjamas more like,' said George. 'You ought to see them. Black nylon they are with a karate top. Cor!'

'Keep the party clean, George.'

'What's it to be then, gentlemen?' said the barman patiently. 'Same again?'

'Same again, Bill, and have one yourself. No, Jack, man is a monogamous animal and there's no partnership on earth to touch a happy marriage. Especially when you're starting off on the right foot like you and Marilyn. Bit of money in the Post Office, nice little flat and nothing to reproach yourselves with.'

'You reckon?' Jack was in a hurry to gloss over that right foot and reproaching stuff. The chairman's homily called to mind the short—but too long—talk he and Marilyn had suffered two days before in the vicar's

study. He downed his beer, looking around him
uncomfortably.

'The first ten years are the worst,' he heard someone
say, and he turned, suddenly nettled. 'Well, damn it,'
he said, 'you are a bloody cheerful mob. I notice it's
the bachelors who don't have a good word to say for
marriage.'

'That's right,' the chairman concurred. 'Pity there
aren't a few more husbands to back me up, eh, Jack?
Charlie Hatton now. There's an us-ux-what's the word
I want?'

'Don't ask me. What the hell does it matter, anyway?
You and your words. This is supposed to be a stag
party, not an annual general meeting. What we need is
someone to liven things up.'

'Like Charlie. Where d'you reckon he's got to?'

'He said he'd be late. He's bringing the lorry down
from Leeds.'

'Maybe he's gone home first.'

'He wouldn't do that. The last thing he said to me on
Wednesday, "Jack," he said, "I'll get along to your
rave-up on Friday even if I have to knock the guts out
of her. I've told Lilian to expect me when she sees
me." No, he'll come here first all right.'

'I hope nothing's happened to him, that's all.'

'Like what?'

'Well, he's had that lorry hi-jacked twice, hasn't he?'

'Bloody old woman you are, George,' said Jack, but
he too had begun to feel uneasy. It was nine-thirty,
only an hour to go before the Dragon closed. Charlie
was going to be his best man. Marvellous wedding he'd
have if they found his best man at midnight somewhere
in the Midlands with his head bashed in.

'Drink up,' said the darts club wit, 'and I'll tell you
the one about the girl who married the sailor.'

'I've heard it,' Jack said dolefully.

'Not this one you haven't. Same again, please, Bill.
There was this girl, you see, and the night before she
got married her mother said, "Now whatever you do,
don't let him . . ."'

for rubbing people up the wrong way. Funny *he* never fell foul of him. 'My round, I think.'

'Can't have that, Jack. Seven more doubles, Bill. Jack, I said *put it away*. I can afford it. There's plenty more where that came from. I come in late, didn't I, so I've got lee-way to make up?'

'No more for me,' said the man whose joke Charlie had spoiled. He patted Jack's shoulder and said good night while the others drank their whisky in an awkward silence.

'Last orders, gentlemen, please,' said the barman.

George Carter dipped his hand into his pocket and brought out some small silver. 'One for the road then, Jack?'

Charlie looked at the little coins. 'What's that? Your missus's housekeeping?'

George flushed. He wasn't married; Charlie knew he wasn't married; knew moreover that his steady had chucked him two weeks before. George had got the deposit ready for a house and made the first down payment on a dining suite. 'You bastard,' he said.

Charlie bristled at him, a smart little fighting cock.

'Nobody calls me a bastard.'

'Gentlemen, gentlemen,' said the barman.

'Yes,' said the chairman, 'pack it in. Talk about folks being touchy, Charlie. No wonder they're touchy when you pick on them the way you do.' He smiled breezily, struck an orator's attitude. 'Now the evening's drawing to a close, and I reckon we ought to take the opportunity of conveying to Jack here the heartiest good wishes of the Kingsmarkham and District Darts Club. I for one . . .'

'We'll take it as said then, shall we?' said Charlie. 'A hearty vote of thanks for the chairman.' He put another fiver on the counter. As red as George had been, the chairman shrugged and gave Jack a nod which was meaningful and sympathetic but which Jack ignored. Then he went, taking another man with him.

The barman wiped the counter in silence. Charlie Hatton had always been cocky but in the past weeks he'd become insufferable and most of the meetings had broken up like this.

Of the stag party now only Jack, Charlie, George and one other remained. He was a lorry driver like Charlie, his name was Maurice Cullam and until now he had scarcely opened his mouth except to pour alcohol down it. Now, having witnessed the rout and ignominy of his friends, he took his last drink and said:

'Been seeing much of McCloy lately, Charlie?'

Charlie made no reply and it was Jack who said, 'Why, have you?'

'Not me, Jack. I keep my hands clean. Money's not everything. I like to sleep quiet in my bed.'

Instead of the expected explosion, Charlie said softly and mildly, 'Time you did. Time you slept for a change.'

Maurice had five children born in six years. Charlie's crack could be taken as a compliment and as such, to the relief of George and Jack, Maurice took it. He smiled sheepishly at this tribute to his virility. Considering Maurice's wife was an exceptionally plain woman, there were a good many ripostes Charlie could have made, ripostes which might have been transparently insulting. Instead he had chosen to flatter.

'Time, gentlemen,' said the barman. 'Here's wishing you all you wish yourself, Mr Pertwee.' The barman usually called Jack by his Christian name and Jack knew 'Mr Pertwee' was a mark never to be repeated, of the respect due to a bridegroom.

'Thanks a lot,' he said, 'and for a grand evening. I'll be seeing you.'

'Let's be toddling, Jack,' said Charlie, and he tucked his fat wallet away.

The air was soft and mild and the sky scattered with many stars. Orion rode above them, his belt crossed by a wrack of midsummer cloud.

'Lovely night,' said Charlie. 'Going to be a fine day tomorrow, Jack.'

'You think?'

'Happy is the bride that the sun shines on.' Drink

had made George sentimental and he turned his mouth down lugubriously as he remembered his steady and the down payment on the furniture.

'You have a good cry, mate,' said Charlie. 'Nothing like a bit of a weep to make a girl feel better.'

George led the Kingsmarkham group of Morris dancers and in the past Charlie had fripped him when he appeared in his motley suit, his cap and bells. He bit his lip, clenching his fists. Then he shrugged and turned away. 'Get stuffed,' he muttered. The others watched him cross the road and make his unsteady way down York Street. Jack raised one hand in a feeble salute.

'You shouldn't have said that, Charlie.'

'Ah, he makes me sick. Let's have a bit of a sing-song then, shall we?' He put one arm around Jack's waist and the other, after a barely discernible pause, around Maurice's.

'One of them old music-hall ballads of yours, Charlie.'

They meandered along under the old overhanging house fronts and Jack had to duck his head to avoid cracking it on a lamp in an iron cage. Charlie cleared his throat and sang:

> 'Mabel dear, listen here!
> There's robbery in the park.
> I sat alone in the Y.M.C.A.,
> Singing just like a lark—
> There's no place like ho-ome,
> But I couldn't go home in the dark!'

'Yoo-hoo!' yelled Jack in Wild Western imitation, but his voice tailed away as Inspector Burden of Kingsmarkham C.I.D. emerged from Queen Street and approached them across the forecourt of the Olive and Dove. ''Evening, Mr. Burden.'

''Evening.' The inspector viewed them with cool distaste. 'We wouldn't want to do anything likely to lead to a breach of the peace, would we?' He passed on and Charlie Hatton sniggered.

'Copper,' he said. 'I reckon I've got more in this pocket than he gets in a month.'

Maurice said stiffly, 'I'll say good night then, Jack.' They had come to the Kingsbrook bridge and the beginning of the footpath to Sewingbury that followed the waters of the river. Maurice lived in Sewingbury, Charlie in one of the new council flats on the far side of the Kingsbrook Road. The footpath was a short cut home for both of them.

'Wait for Charlie. He's going your way.'

'I won't, thanks. I promised the missus I'd be home by eleven.' Charlie had turned his back, making it plain he didn't want Maurice's company. 'Powerful stuff, that,' Maurice said, his face pale in the lamplight. 'I don't reckon I should have mixed it.' He belched and Charlie sniggered. 'Cheers, Jack, see you in church.'

'Cheers, mate.'

Maurice vaulted the stile and, by a miracle, landed steadily on his feet. He passed the wooden seats, ducked under the willows, and the last they saw of him was his undulating shadow. Jack and Charlie were alone.

They had drunk a great deal and the night was warm, but on a sudden they were both stone-cold sober. Both of them loved women and in that love as in every emotion they were inarticulate, yet in no impulse of the heart were they so tongue-tied as in this great and pure friendship of theirs.

As with the Greeks, they had found in each other an all-embracing spiritual compatibility. Their women were their pride and treasure, for bed, for hearth and home, for showing off, for their manhood. But without each other their lives would be incomplete, lacking, as it were, the essence and the fuse. They had never heard of the Greeks, unless you counted the man who kept the Acropolis restaurant in Stowerton, and neither could now understand the emotion which held each of them, preserving him in silence and a kind of despair.

If Charlie had been a different man, a cultivated man or effeminate or living in a bygone age when tongues were more freely unloosed, he might now have embraced Jack and told him from a full heart how he entered wholly into his joy and would die for his happiness. And if Jack had been such another he would have thanked Charlie for his unstinted friendship, his generous loans, his hospitality and for bringing him Marilyn Thompson. But Charlie was a sharp little lorry driver and Jack was an electrician. Love was between a man and a woman, love was for marriage, and each would have died before admitting to anything more than that they 'got on well' together. They hung over the bridge, dropping stone chippings into the water, and then Charlie said:

'I reckon you need your beauty sleep, so I'll be on my way.'

'We got your present, Charlie. I wasn't going to say nothing till the others had gone, but it's a real grand job that recordplayer. It quite knocked me back when I saw it. Must have set you back a bit.'

'I got it at cost, mate.' Another stone dropped and splashed in the darkness beneath.

'Marilyn said she'd be writing to Lilian.'

'She has, too. A lovely letter come from her before I went up north. A real educated girl you got there, Jack. She knows how to put a letter together all right. You don't grudge the outlay when you get a letter like that. I brought you two together and don't you ever forget it.'

'Ah, you know how to pick them, Charlie. Look at Lilian.'

'Well, I'd better get looking at her, hadn't I?' Charlie turned to face his friend and his shadow was short and black against Jack's long one. He raised his hard little hand and brought it down on Jack's resoundingly. 'I'll be off, then.'

'I reckon you'd better, Charlie.'

'And if I don't get the chance tomorrow—well, I'm no speechmaker like Brian, but all the very best, Jack.'

'You'll get the chance all right. You'll have to make a speech.'

'Save it up till then, eh?' Charlie wrinkled his nose and winked quickly. The shadows parted, he negotiated the stile. 'Good night, me old love.'

' 'Night, Charlie.'

The willows enclosed him. His shadow appeared again as the path rose and dipped. Jack heard him whistling. 'Mabel dear, listen here' under the stars and then as the shadow was absorbed and lost in the many tree shadows, the whistle too faded and there was no sound but the gentle chatter of the stream, the Kingsbrook that flowed everlastingly over its bed of thin round stones.

Many waters cannot quench love, nor the floods drown it.

2

DETECTIVE CHIEF INSPECTOR Wexford didn't care for dogs. He had never had a dog and now that one of his daughters was married and the other a student at drama school, he saw no reason why he should ever give one house-room. Many an anti-dog man joins the ranks of dog lovers because he is too weak to resist the demands of beloved children, but in Wexford's household the demands had never been more than half-hearted, so he had passed through this snare and come out unscathed.

When therefore he arrived home late on Friday night to find the grey thing with ears like knitted dishcloths in his favourite chair he was displeased.

'Isn't she a darling?' said the drama student. 'Her

name's Clytemnestra. I knew you wouldn't mind having her for just a fortnight.' And she whisked out to answer the telephone.

'Where did Sheila get it from?' Wexford said gloomily.

Mrs. Wexford was a woman of few words.

'Sebastian.'

'Who in God's name is Sebastian?'

'Some boy,' said Mrs. Wexford. 'He's only just gone.'

Her husband considered pushing the dog on to the floor, thought better of it, and went sulkily off to bed. His daughter's beauty had never ceased to surprise the chief inspector. Sylvia, the elder married one, was well-built and healthy, but that was the best that could be said for her; Mrs. Wexford had a magnificent figure and a fine profile although she had never been of the stuff that wins beauty contests. While he . . . All he needed, he sometimes thought, was a trunk to make him look exactly like an elephant. His body was huge and ponderous, his skin pachydermatous, wrinkled and grey, and his three-cornered ears stuck out absurdly under the sparse fringe of colourless hair. When he went to the zoo he passed the elephant house quickly lest the irreverent onlooker should make comparisons.

Her mother and sister were fine-looking women, but the odd thing about Sheila was that her beauty was not an enlargement or an enhancement of their near-handsomeness. She looked like her father. The first time Wexford noticed this—she was then about six—he almost hooted aloud, so grotesque was the likeness between this exquisite piece of doll's flesh and her gross progenitor. And yet, that high broad forehead was his, the little tilted nose was his, his the pointed—although in her case, flat—ears, and in her huge grey eyes he saw his own little ones. When he was young his hair had been that flaxen gold too, as soft and as fine. Only hope she doesn't end up looking like her dad, he thought with a rich inner guffaw.

But on the following morning his feelings towards his younger daughter were neither tender nor amused.

The dog had awakened him at ten to seven with long-drawn howls and now, a quarter of an hour later, he stood on the threshold of Sheila's bedroom, glowering.

'This isn't a boarding kennels, you know,' he said. 'Can't you hear her?'

'The Acrylic Swoofle Hound, Pop? Poor darling, she only wants to be taken out.'

'What did you call her?'

'The Acrylic Swoofle Hound. She's a mongrel really, but that's what Sebastian calls her. She looks as if she's made of man-made fibres you see. Don't you think it's funny?'

'Not particularly. Why can't this Sebastian look after his own dog?'

'He's gone to Switzerland,' said Sheila. 'His plane must have gone by now.' She surfaced from under the sheets and her father saw that her hair was wound on huge electrically heated rollers. 'I felt awful letting him walk all that way to the station last night.' She added accusingly, 'But you had the car.'

'It's my car,' Wexford almost shouted. This argument he knew of old was hopeless and he listened to his own voice with a kind of horror as a note of pleading crept into it. 'If the dog wants to go out, hadn't you better get up and take her?'

'I can't. I've just set my hair.' Downstairs Clytemnestra let out a howl that ended in a series of urgent yelps. Sheila threw back the bedclothes and sat up, a vision in pink baby doll pyjamas.

'God almighty!' Wexford exploded. 'You can't take your friend's dog out but you can get up at the crack of dawn to set your hair.'

'Daddy . . . .' The wheedling tone as well as the now seldom-used paternal appellation told Wexford that a monstrous request was to be made of him. He glared, drawing his brows together in the manner that made Kingsmarkham's petty offenders tremble. 'Daddy, duck, it's a gorgeous morning and you know what Dr. Crocker said about your weight and I *have* just set my hair . . .'

'I am going to take a shower,' Wexford said coldly.

He took it. When he emerged from the bathroom the dog was still howling and pop music was issuing from behind Sheila's door. A degenerate male voice exhorted its hearers to give it love or let it die in peace.

'There seems to be an awful lot of noise going on, darling,' said Mrs. Wexford sleepily.

'You're joking.'

He opened Sheila's door. She was applying a face pack.

'Just this once, then,' said the chief inspector. 'I'm only doing it because I want your mother to have a quiet lie-in, so you can turn that thing off for a start.'

"You are an angel, Daddy,' said Sheila, and she added dreamily, 'I expect Clytemnestra has spent a penny by now.'

Clytemnestra. Of all the stupid pretentious names for a dog . . . But what else could you expect of someone called Sebastian? She had not, however, yet 'spent a penny'. She flung herself on Wexford, yelping frenetically, and when he pushed her away, ran round him in circles, wildly gyrating her tail and flapping her knitted ears.

Wexford found the lead, obligingly left by Sheila in a prominent position on top of the refrigerator. Undoubtedly it was going to be a beautiful day, a summer's day such as is unequalled anywhere in the world but in the South of England, a day that begins with mists, burgeons into tropical glory and dies in blue and gold and stars.

'Full many a glorious morning,' quoted Wexford to Clytemnestra, 'have I seen, flatter the mountain tops with sovereign eye.'

Clytemnestra agreed vociferously, leaping on to a stool and screeching hysterically at sight of her lead.

'Bear your body more seemly,' said Wexford coldly, switching from sonnet to comedy without varying his author. He looked out of the window. The sovereign eye was there all right, bright, molten and white-gold.

Instead of mountain tops it was flattering the
Kingsbrook meadows and turning the little river into a
ribbon of shimmering metal. It wouldn't do him any
harm to take this ungoverned creature for a short jaunt
in the fields and the experience would give him a splendid ascendancy over Inspector Burden when he walked
into the station at nine-thirty.

'Lovely morning, sir.'

'It was, Mike. The best of it's over now, of course.
Now when I was down by the river at half seven . . .'

He chuckled. Clytemnestra whimpered. Wexford
went to the door and the dog screamed for joy. He
clipped on the lead and stepped forth into the sweet
peace of a summer Saturday in Sussex.

It was one thing to boast afterwards of pre-breakfast
hiking, quite another to be actually seen leading this
freak of nature, this abortion, about the public streets.
Observed in uncompromising midsummer light,
Clytemnestra looked like something that, having long
lain neglected at the bottom of an old woman's knitting
basket, has finally been brought out to be mended.

Moreover, now that she had achieved the heart's desire for which she had turned on her shameless, neur-
otic display, she had become dejected, and walked
along meekly, head and tail hanging. Just like a woman, Wexford thought crossly. Sheila would be just the
same. Hair out of curlers, face cleaned up, she was in
all probability downstairs now calmly making her
mother a cup of tea. When you get what you want you
don't want what you get. . . . *On a fait le monde ainsi.*

He would, however, eschew the public streets.

From this side of town, the footpath led across the
fields to the bank of the stream where it divided, one
branch going to the new council estate and Sewingbury,
the other to the centre of Kingsmarkham High Street,
at the Kingsbrook bridge. Wexford certainly wasn't
going to embark on a sabbath day's journey to Sewingbury, and now they had mucked up the Kingsbrook
Road with those flats, there was no longer any point

in going there. Instead he would walk down to the river, take the path to the bridge and pick up his *Police Review* at Braddan's on his way home. They always forgot to send it with the papers.

In agricultural districts pastureland is usually fenced. These meadows were divided by hedges and barbed wire and in them great red cattle were grazing. Mist lay in shallow patches over the hollows and where the fields were lying fallow the hay was nearly ready to be cut, but it was not yet cut. Wexford, very much a countryman at heart, marvelled that the townsman calls grass green when in reality it is as many-coloured as Joseph's coat. The grass heads hung heavy with seed, ochre, chestnut and powdery grey, and all the thick tapestry of pasture was embroidered and interlaced with the crimson thread of sorrel, the bright acid of buttercups and the creamy dairymaid floss of meadow-sweet. Over it all the fanning whispering seed and the tenuous mist cast a sheen of silver.

The oak trees had not yet lost the vivid yellow-green of their late springtime, a colour so bright, so fresh and so unparalleled elsewhere in nature or in art that no one has ever been able to emulate it and it is never seen in paint or cloth or women's dresses. In such things the colour would be crude, if it could be copied, but against this pale blue yet fixedly cloudless sky it was not crude. It was exquisite. Wexford drew in lungfuls of scented, pollen-laden air. He never had hay fever and he felt good.

The dog, who had perhaps feared a pavement perambulation, sniffed the air too and became frisky. She poked about in the brambles and wagged her tail. Wexford undid the lead clip and let her run.

With a kind of stolid tranquillity he began to reflect on the day's work ahead. That grievous bodily harm thing was coming up at a special court this morning, but that ought to be all wrapped up in half an hour. Then there was the possibility of the silver on sale at the Saturday morning market being stolen goods. Someone had better go down and have a word. . . . No

doubt there'd been the usual spate of Friday night bur-
glaries, too.

Mrs. Fanshawe had regained consciousness in Stowerton Royal Infirmary after her six-week-long coma.
They would have to talk to her today. But that was the
uniformed branch's pigeon, not his. Thank God, it
wasn't he who had to break the news to the woman
that her husband and her daughter had both been
killed in the car crash that had fractured her skull.

Presumably they would now resume the adjourned
inquest on that unfortunate pair. Burden said Mrs.
Fanshawe might just recall why her husband's Jaguar
had skidded and overturned on the empty fast lane of
the twin track road, but he doubted it. A merciful am-
nesia usually came with these comas and who could
deny it was a blessing? It seemed downright immoral to
torment the poor woman with questions now just for
the sake of proving the Jaguar's brakes were faulty or
Fanshawe driving over the seventy limit. It wasn't as if
any other vehicle had been involved. No doubt there
was some question of insurance. Anyway, it wasn't his
worry.

The sun shone on the rippling river and the long willow leaves just touched its bubbling golden surface. A
trout jumped for a sparkling iridescent fly. Clytemnestra went down to the water and drank greedily. In this
world of clean fast-running water, of inimitable oaks
and meadows which made the Bayeux tapestry look
like a traycloth, there was no place for somersaulted
cars and carnage and broken bodies lying on the wet
and bloody tarmac.

The dog paddled, then swam. In the sunshine even
grey knitted Clytemnestra was beautiful. Beneath her
flat furry belly the big shallow stones had the marble
veining of agate. Upon the water the mist floated in a
golden veil, spotted with the dancing of a myriad tiny
flies. And Wexford who was an agnostic, a profane
man, thought, Lord, how manifold are thy works in all
the earth.

There was a man on the other side of the river. He was walking slowly some fifty yards from the opposite bank and parallel to it, walking from the Sewingbury direction to Kingsmarkham. A child was with him, holding his hand, and he too had a dog, a big pugnacious-looking black dog. Wexford had an idea, drawn partly from experience in looking out of his office window, that when two dogs meet they inevitably fight. Clytemnestra would come out badly from a fight with that big black devil. Wexford couldn't bring himself to call his charge by her name. He whistled.

Clytemnestra took no notice. She had gained the opposite bank and was poking about in a great drifting mass of torn grass and brushwood. Further upstream a cache of rubbish had been washed against the bank. Wexford, who had been lyrical, felt positively pained by this evidence of man's indifference to nature's glories. He could see a bundle of checked cloth, an old blanket perhaps, an oil drum and, a little apart from the rest, a floating shoe. Clytemnestra confirmed his low opinion of everything canine by advancing on this water-logged pocket of rubbish, her tail wagging and her ears pricked. Filthy things, dogs, Wexford thought, scavengers and dustbin delvers. He whistled again. The dog stopped and he was just about to congratulate himself on his authoritative and successful method of summoning her, when she made a plunging dart forward and seized the mass of cloth in her mouth.

It moved with a heavy surge and the dog released it, her hackles rising. The slow and somehow primeval erecting of that mat of grey hairs brought a curious chill to Wexford's blood. The sun seemed to go in. He forgot the black dog, coming ever nearer, and his joy in the morning went. Clytemnestra let out an unearthly keening howl, her lips snarling back and her tail a stiff prolongation of her backbone.

The bundle she had disturbed eddied a few inches into the deeper water and as Wexford watched, a thin pale hand, lifeless as the agate-veined stones, rose slowly from the sodden cloth, its fingers hanging, yet pointing towards him.

He took off his shoes and socks and rolled his trousers to his knees. The man and the child on the other side watched him with interest. He didn't think they had yet seen the hand. Holding his shoes, he stepped on to the stones and crossed the river carefully. Clytemnestra came to him quickly and put her face against his bare leg. Wexford pushed aside the willows that hung like a pelmet and came to the rubbish pocket, where he knelt down. One shoe floated empty, the other was still on a foot. The dead man lay facedownwards and someone had smashed in the back of his head with a heavy smooth object. One of these very stones, Wexford guessed.

The brambles shivered behind him and a footstep crunched.

'Keep back,' Wexford said. 'Keep the child back.'

He turned, shielding what lay in the water with his own big body. Downstream the child was playing with both dogs, throwing stones for them into the water.

'Christ!' said the man softly.

'He's dead,' said Wexford. 'I'm a police officer and . . .'

'I know you. Chief Inspector Wexford.' The man approached and Wexford couldn't stop him. He looked down and gasped. 'My God, I . . .'

'Yes, it isn't a pleasant sight.' The thought came to Wexford that something very out of the way had happened. Not so much that here on a fine June morning a man lay murdered, but that he, Wexford, had found him. Policemen don't find bodies unless they are sent to look for them or unless someone else has found them first. 'Will you do something for me?' he asked. The newcomer's face was green. He looked as if he was about to be sick. 'Will you go down to the town, to the nearest phone box and get on to the station? Just tell them what you've seen. They'll do the rest. Come on, man, pull yourself together.'

'O.K., it's just that . . .'

'Perhaps you'd better let me have your name.'

'Cullam, Maurice Cullam. I'll go. I'll go right away. It's just that—well, last night I was having a drink with him at the Dragon.'

'You know who it is then? You can't see his face.'

'I don't need to. I'd know Charlie Hatton anywhere.'

3

He looked a right Charlie in those tails and striped trousers. That would be something funny to say to his best man when he came.

'You and me, we look a pair of right Charlies, Charlie Hatton.'

Quite witty really. Jack often thought he wasn't quick enough to match Charlie's easy repartee, but now he had thought of something that would make his friend smile.

Dear old Charlie, he thought sentimentally, the best friend a man ever had. Generous to a fault, and if he wasn't always strictly above-board—well, a man had to live. And Charlie knew how to live all right. The best of everything he had. Jack was ready to bet all the crisp honeymoon pound notes he had in his pocket that Charlie would be one of the few guests not wearing a hired morning coat. He had his own and not off the peg, either.

Not that he looked half bad himself, he thought, admiring his reflection. At his age boozing didn't have much visible effect and he always had a red face anyway. He looked smashing, he decided, shyly proud, as

good as the Duke of Edinburgh any day. Probably the
Duke used an electric shaver though. Jack put another
bit of cotton wool on the nick on his chin and he wondered if Marilyn was ready yet.

Thanks to Charlie boy, they'd been able to splash a
bit on the wedding and Marilyn could have the white
satin and the four bridesmaids she'd set her heart on. It
would have been a different story if they'd had to find
the key money for the flat themselves. Trust Charlie to
come up with a long-term interest-free loan. That way
they'd be able to blue some of their own savings on
having the flat done up nicely. How well it had all
worked out! A fortnight away by the sea and when
they came back, the flat all ready and waiting for them.
And it was all thanks to Charlie.

Moving away from the mirror, Jack looked into the
future, twenty, thirty years hence. Charlie would be a
really rich man by then. Jack would be very much surprised if his friend wouldn't be living in one of those
houses in Ploughman's Lane like the one where he
sometimes did electrical jobs with real old French furniture and real oil paintings and the kind of china you
looked at but didn't eat off. He and Charlie had had a
good laugh over that particular house, but there had
been something serious in Charlie's laughter and Jack
had guessed he aimed high.

They'd still be mates of course, for there was no side
to Charlie Hatton. It wouldn't be beer and a hand of
solo then, but dinner parties and bridge games and with
their wives in cocktail gowns and real jewellery. Jack
grew dizzy as he thought of it, seeing them sitting with
tall glasses on a shady patio and, strangely, seeing them
too as they were now, untouched by the hand of time.

Abruptly he came back to the present day, his wedding day. Charlie was taking a hell of a time about
coming. Maybe there was some difficulty about Lilian's
dress or he was waiting for her to get back from the
hairdresser's. Charlie was dead keen on Lilian doing
him credit and she always did, always looked as if
she'd just stepped out of a bandbox. After Marilyn,

she'd be the best dressed woman at the wedding, blonde, shapely, in the green dress Marilyn had got so superstitious about. Jack dabbed at his chin again and went to the window to watch for Charlie.

It was ten-thirty and the wedding was fixed for an hour's time.

She was blonde, shapely, pretty in Sheila Wexford's style but without Sheila's transcending beauty. Her face was rather blunt, the features unfinished putty dabs, and now it was swollen with crying. After they had told her Wexford and Burden sat helplessly while she flung herself face-downwards on the sofa and sobbed into the cushions.

Presently Wexford moved over to her and touched her shoulder. She reached for his hand, clutched it and dug in her long nails. Then she struggled up, burying her face in his hand and her own. The expensive velvet cushions were blotched with her tears.

Wexford glanced quickly around the smartly, even luxuriously, furnished room. Over the back of one of the chairs hung a blue and green flowered dress, a green coat, long wrist-buttoning gloves. In the middle of the long teak dining table lay Lilian Hatton's wedding hat, an elaborate confection of satin leaves and tulle as green and fresh as the real leaves he could see through the picture window in the Kingsbrook meadows.

'Mrs. Hatton,' he said gently and she raised her face obediently, 'Mrs. Hatton, weren't you worried when your husband didn't come home last night?'

She didn't speak. He repeated the question, and then she said in a voice choked with sobs, 'I didn't expect him home. I only half-expected him.' She dropped Wexford's hand, recoiling as if in taking it she had done something indecent.

'When he didn't come,' she said, 'I thought He hasn't made it, he hasn't made Jack's party. He's stopping off on the road, he'll be in in the morning. I . . .' The sobs were uncontrollable and she gave a long piteous cry.

'I won't trouble you any more now, Mrs. Hatton. You say your mother's coming? If I could just have Mr. Pertwee's address . . .'

'Jack, yes,' she said. 'Jack'll take this hard.' She drew a long breath, twisting her hands. 'They'd been pals since they were schoolkids.' Suddenly she stood up, staring wildly. 'God, Jack doesn't know! It's his wedding day and Charlie was going to be his best man. Oh, Jack, Jack, poor Jack!'

'Leave it to us, Mrs. Hatton,' said Inspector Burden. 'We'll tell Mr. Pertwee. Bailey Street, is it? We'll tell him. There's your front door bell now. I expect that'll be your mother.'

'Mum,' said Lilian Hatton. 'What am I going to do, Mum?' The older woman looked past her, then put her arms around the shaking shoulders. 'Marilyn said I shouldn't wear green to a wedding, she said it was unlucky.' Her voice was very low, a slurring mumble. 'I bought that green coat just the same. I never got as far as the wedding, Mum, but it was unlucky, wasn't it?' Suddenly she broke into a terrible, loud and demented scream. 'Charlie, Charlie, what am I going to do, Charlie?' She held on to her mother, clawing at the lapels of her coat. 'Oh my God, Charlie!' she screamed.

'I never get used to it, you know,' said Burden quietly.

'Do you think I do?' Wexford had amiable, sometimes distinctly fond feelings for his subordinate, but occasionally Burden made him impatient, especially when he instituted himself keeper of the chief inspector's conscience. He had a smug parsonical face, Wexford thought unkindly, and now his thin mouth turned piously down. 'The worst is over anyway,' he said crossly. 'The bridegroom won't go into transports of grief and you don't put off your wedding because your best man's been done in.'

You callous devil, said Burden's look. Then the neat,

well-modelled head was once more averted and the inspector reentered his silent, respectful reverie.

It took only ten minutes to get from the Hattons' flat to Bailey Street where, at number ten, Jack Pertwee lived with his widowed father. The police car stopped outside a tiny terraced house with no garden to separate its front door from the pavement. Mr. Pertwee senior answered their knock, looking uneasy in a too large morning coat.

'Thought you were our missing best man come at last.'

'I'm afraid Mr. Hatton won't be coming, sir.' Wexford and Burden edged themselves courteously but firmly past him into the narrow hall. 'I'm very sorry to tell you we have bad news.'

'Bad news?'

'Yes, sir, Mr. Hatton died last night. He was found down by the river this morning and he'd been dead since midnight or before.'

Pertwee went pale as chalk. 'By gum,' he said, 'Jack'll take this hard.' His mouth trembling, he looked at them both and then down at the knife-edge creases in his trousers. 'D'you want me to go up and tell him?' Wexford nodded. 'Well, if that's the way you want it. He's getting married at eleven-thirty. But if I've got to tell him, I suppose I've got to tell him.'

They both knew Jack Pertwee by sight. Most Kingsmarkham faces were familiar to Wexford and Burden remembered seeing him the night before arm-in-arm with the dead man, singing and disturbing decent citizens. A happily married man himself, he had the deepest sympathy for the widow, but in his heart he thought Jack Pertwee a bit of a lout. You didn't have to tread softly with such as he and he wondered scornfully why the fellow's face was lard-coloured.

Impatiently he watched him lumber blindly down the steep narrow staircase and when the bridegroom reached the bottom, Burden said curtly:

'Your father's told you? Hatton was murdered last

night. We want to know the lot, where you'd been and what time you left him.'

'Here, go easy,' said the father. 'It's been a shock. They were old mates, my boy and Charlie.'

Jack pushed past him into the poky front parlour and the others followed. The wedding flowers had come. Jack had a white rose in his buttonhole and there were two more, their stems wrapped in silver foil, on the fumed oak sideboard. One was for the bridegroom's father and the other would never be worn. Jack plucked the flower out of his morning coat and closed his fist slowly over it, crushing it into a pulp.

'I'll get you a drop of whisky, son.'

'I don't want it,' Jack said with his back to them. 'We was drinking whisky last night. I never want to touch it again.' He pulled his black immaculate sleeve across his eyes. 'Who did it?' he shouted.

'We hoped you'd be able to tell us that,' said Burden.

'Me? Are you out of your bloody mind? Just show me the bastard who killed Charlie Hatton and I'll . . . .' He sat down heavily, spread his arms on the table and dropped his head.

'Charlie,' he said.

Wexford didn't pursue it. He turned to the father. 'What was it last night, a stag party?' Pertwee nodded. 'D'you know who was there?'

'Jack, of course, and poor old Charlie. Then there was all the darts club lot, George Carter, fellow called Bayles, Maurice Cullam from Sewingbury and a couple of others. That right, Jack?'

Jack nodded dumbly.

'Charlie got there late, Jack said. They left at closing time, split up outside, I reckon. Charlie and Cullam'll have walked home across the fields. That right, Jack?'

This time Jack lifted his head. Burden thought him a weak womanish fool, despising his red eyes and the muscle that twitched in his cheek. But Wexford spoke gently.

'I realise this has been a blow to you, Mr. Pertwee.

We won't bother you much longer. Did Mr. Cullam and Mr. Hatton walk home together?'

'Maurice went first,' Jack muttered. 'About twenty to eleven it was. Charlie . . . Charlie stayed for a bit of a natter with me.' A sob caught his throat and he coughed to mask it. 'He said he wished me luck in case he didn't get a chance today. Christ, he didn't know he'd never get another chance.'

'Come on, son, bear up. Let me give you a little drop of scotch. You owe it to Marilyn to keep going you know. It's your wedding day, remember?'

Jack shook off his father's hand and lurched to his feet.

'There isn't going to be no wedding,' he said.

'You don't mean that, Jack, think of that girl of yours, think of all them folks coming. They'll be getting to the church in a minute. Charlie wouldn't have wished it.'

Stubbornly Jack said, 'I'm not getting married today. D'you think I don't know what's right, what's proper?' He wrenched off his tie and flung his morning coat over the back of a chair.

His father, with a working man's regard for hired finery, picked it up, smoothed it and stood draping it over his arm like an outfitter's assistant. Bewildered by the holocaust of events, by death that had suddenly changed a world, he began apologising, first to the policemen: 'I don't know what to say, his best man to die like that . . .' and then to his son: 'I'd give my right hand to have things different, Jack. What can I do for you, son? I'll do anything you say.'

Jack dropped his handful of bruised petals. A sudden dignity made him straighten his back and hold his head high. 'Then get down to that church,' he said, 'and tell them the wedding's off.' He faced Wexford. 'I'm not answering any more questions now. I've got my grief. You ought to respect my grief.' Still the old man hesitated, biting his lip. 'Go on, Dad,' Jack said fiercely. 'Tell them it's all off and tell them why.' He gasped as if suddenly, at this moment, it had come home to him. 'Tell them Charlie Hatton's dead!'

Oh, Jonathan, thou wast slain in thy high places . . . How are the mighty fallen and the weapons of war perished!

'A best man, indeed,' said Burden. 'Everyone's best man.'

You callous devil, thought Wexford. 'Naturally Pertwee'd be upset. What did you expect?'

Burden made a moue of disgust. 'That sort of grief, that's the widow's province. A man ought to have more self-control.' His pale ascetic face flushed unbecomingly. 'You don't suppose there was anything . . .?'

'No, I don't,' said Wexford. 'And why can't you call a spade a spade? They were friends. Don't you have friends, Mike? A pretty pass we've come to if a man can't have a friend without being labelled queer.' He stared aggressively at Burden and declaimed loudly and meaningfully, 'O brave new world, that has such people in it!'

Burden gave a stiff repressive cough and maintained silence until they reached York Street. Then he said coldly, 'George Carter's place is down here, old Pertwee said.'

'He's the Morris dancer, isn't he? I've seen him cavorting about on summer nights outside the Olive and Dove.'

'Lot of affected nonsense.'

But George Carter wasn't wearing his cap and bells this morning. From the brilliantined hair and the smart lounge suit, Wexford gathered that here was a wedding guest.

He hinted at the unlikelihood of Jack Pertwee's being married that day and was inwardly amused to observe that this piece of information—the fact that Carter would be deprived of his cold chicken and champagne—distressed him more than Hatton's death.

The wedding guest did not exactly beat his breast but he looked considerably crestfallen.

'All that money wasted,' he said. 'I know, I was making plans for my own wedding, but then you won't want to know about that. Pity Jack had to be told, really. I don't seem to be able to take it in. Charlie Hatton dead! He was always so full of life, if you know what I mean.'

'And very well liked, I gather.'

George Carter's eyebrows went up. 'Charlie? Oh well, mustn't speak ill of the dead.'

'You'd better speak the truth, Mr. Carter,' said Burden, 'and never mind whether it's ill or not. We want to know all about this party last night. The lot, please. You can take your time.'

Like Jack Pertwee and yet utterly unlike him, Carter took off his jacket and loosened his tie. 'I don't know what you mean by the lot,' he said. 'It was just a bunch of mates having a drink.'

'What happened? What did you talk about?'

'O.K.' He gave them an incredulous glance and said sarcastically, 'Stop me if I'm boring you. Charlie come into the Dragon at about half nine, maybe a quarter to ten. We was drinking beer so, of course, Charlie has to make us all feel small by paying for whiskies all round. A crack hand at that, was Charlie Hatton. I made some comment and he bit my head off. This the sort of thing you want to know?'

'Exactly the sort of thing, Mr. Carter.'

'Seems a bit mean, that's all, with the poor geezer dead. Then someone else was telling a joke and he sort of—well, humiliated him, if you know what I mean. He was like that, always had to be top dog. He drank my drink because I said something about all the money he was always flashing around and then he made a dirty crack about ... Well, that doesn't matter. It was personal. He got at our chairman too and he left with a couple of the others. Geoff had already gone. There was me and Charlie and Maurice and Jack left and we went when they closed. And that's the lot."

'You're sure?'

'I told you there was nothing much. I can't think of any more . . . Oh, wait a minute. But it was nothing.'

'We'll have it just the same, Mr. Carter.'

George Carter shrugged impatiently. 'I don't even know what it was about. Nothing, I reckon. Maurice said—it was after the others had gone—Maurice said, "Seen much of McCloy lately, Charlie?" I think those were his words. I know the name was McCloy but it didn't mean nothing to me. Jack didn't like it and he was a bit shirty with Maurice. I reckon Charlie looked a bit sick. God, it was all so . . . well, it was nothing. But Charlie'd always rise. I expected him to rise. I don't know why. He didn't. He just made a crack about Maurice needing to sleep quiet in his bed. Said it was time he did, meaning Maurice had so many kids and . . . well, you can get the message.'

'Not altogether,' said Wexford. 'Had Cullam suggested that Hatton couldn't sleep quiet in *his*?'

'That's right. I forget that bit. I wish I could remember his words. Something like "I don't have nothing to do with McCloy, I like to sleep quiet in my bed." '

Very interesting Wexford thought. Far from being popular, Hatton had evidently had a host of enemies. He had spent less than an hour in the Dragon and during that time he had succeeded in needling at least four men.

'You mentioned all the money Hatton used to flash around,' he said. 'What money?'

'He always had wads of it,' said Carter. 'I've known him three years and he was always flush. But he'd had more lately. He bought four rounds of double scotches last night and it didn't even make a hole in what he'd got.'

'How much had he got, Mr. Carter?'

'I didn't count it, you know,' Carter said with asperity. He blew his nose on his clean white wedding handkerchief. 'He'd got his pay packet, but he didn't touch that. Then he had this roll of notes. I told you I didn't count them. How could I?'

'Twenty pounds, thirty, more?'

Carter wrinkled his forehead in an effort of concentration. 'He paid for the first round out of a fiver and the third with another fiver. He'd got two fivers, left, then. As well as that there was a wad of oncers.' He indicated with two parted fingers a quarter of an inch. 'I reckon he was carrying a hundred quid besides his pay.'

4

BY LUNCHTIME WEXFORD and Burden had interviewed all those members of the darts club that had been present at Jack Pertwee's stag party with the exception of Maurice Cullam, but none of them had been able to do more than confirm that Hatton had been aggressive, vain and malicious and that he had been carrying a great deal of money.

They returned to the police station, passing the parish church on whose steps a June bride and her attendants were being photographed. The bridegroom moved out of the throng and Wexford felt a strange sentimental pang because it was not Jack Pertwee. Then he pulled himself together and said, as they mounted the station steps under the concrete canopy:

'Now if we were cops inside the covers of a detective story, Mike, we'd know for sure that Hatton was killed to stop Pertwee getting married today.'

Burden gave a sour smile. 'Easier to kill Pertwee, I'd have thought.'

'Ah, but that's your author's subtlety. Still, we aren't and he wasn't. The chances are he was killed for the money he was carrying. There was nothing in his wallet when I found him.'

The foyer of the police station enclosed them. Behind the long black sweep of counter Sergeant Camb sat fanning himself with a newspaper, the sweat dripping down his forehead. Wexford made for the stairs.

'Why not use the lift, sir?' said Burden.

The police station was not yet half a dozen years old, but ever since its completion the powers that be, like fussy housewives, had been unable to let well alone, adding innovation after innovation, perpetually trying to improve their handiwork. First there had been the stone tubs on the forecourt, a constant temptation to vandals who got a more than commonly satisfying kick from ravishing these particular flowers. Then came the consignment of houseplants for the offices, *tradescantia* and *sanseveria* and *ficus elastica* that were doomed from the start to dehydration and ultimately to have their pots serve as repositories for cigarette ash.

Last year it had been glass sculpture, a strange green tree, a very Ygdrasil, for Burden's sanctum, and for Wexford an inky-blue, amorphous pillar that in some lights grossly resembled the human figure. These, too, had been fated, Wexford's broken by a pretty young woman who was helping him with his enquiries and Burden's one day inadvertently put out with the rubbish.

That should have been the end of it. And then, just as the foyer was beginning to take on a shabby, comfortable look, the lift arrived, an elegant black and gilt box with a sliding door.

'It isn't working yet,' Wexford said, a shade nervously.

'That's where you're wrong. Been operating since this morning. Shall we try it?'

'I should just like to know what's wrong with the stairs,' Wexford exploded. 'It's a downright disgrace wasting the ratepayers' money like this.' He stuck out his lower lip. 'Besides, Crocker says walking upstairs is the best exercise in the world for me with my blood pressure.'

'Just as you like,' said Burden, turning his face away so that Wexford should not see him smile.

By the time they reached the third floor they were both out of breath. The flimsy yellow chair behind Wexford's rosewood desk creaked as he lowered his heavy body into it.

'For God's sake open a window, Mike.'

Burden grumbled that opening windows upset the air conditioning but he complied, raising the yellow venetian blind and letting in a powerful shaft of noonday sunshine.

'Well, sir,' he said. 'Shall we re-cap on what we know about Charlie Hatton?'

'Thirty years old, born and bred in Kingsmarkham. Two years ago he got married to a Miss Lilian Bardsley, sister of the man he's in business with. Bardsley's got his own firm, transporting small electrical goods.'

'Was Hatton a full partner?'

'We'll have to find out. Even if he was, I can't see he could get that flush driving loads of irons and heaters up to Leeds and Scotland a couple of times a week. Carter says he had a hundred quid on him, Mike. Where did he get the money from?'

'Maybe this McCloy.'

'Do we know any McCloys?'

'Not that I can recall, sir. We shall have to ask Maurice Cullam.'

Wexford wiped his brow with his handkerchief and, following Camb's example, began to fan himself with the morning paper. 'The philoprogenitive Cullam,' he said. 'He had one of his quiverful with him when I found Hatton this morning. He's a lorry driver too, Mike. I wonder . . . Hatton had this lorry hi-jacked twice this year.'

Burden opened his pale-blue eyes wide. 'Is that so?'

'I remembered,' said Wexford, 'as soon as Cullam told me whose the body was. Both times were on the Great North Road and no one was ever done for it.

Hatton got knocked on the head the first time but the second time he wasn't hurt, only tied up.'

'Once,' said Burden thoughtfully, 'is fair enough. Occupational hazard. Twice looks fishy. I want to hear what the doctor has to say. And if I'm not mistaken that's him outside now.'

Dr. Crocker and Wexford had been at school together. Like Jack Pertwee and Charlie Hatton, they were lifelong friends, but their friendship was a casual business and their manner to each other dry, irreverent, often caustic. Crocker, some six years the chief inspector's junior, was the only man Burden knew who could get the better of Wexford and match his acid tongue. A tall lean figure with deep lines carved vertically down his brown cheeks, he came into the office looking as cool as he did on a winter's day.

'I used your lift,' said the doctor. 'Very smart. Whatever will they think of next?'

'Pictures are threatened,' said Wexford. 'The inspector here is to have a suitable flower piece and I a Constable landscape.'

'I don't know much about art,' said Crocker, sitting down and crossing one elegant lean leg over the other, 'but there's one painting I *would* like to have. Rembrandt, The Anatomy Lesson. Lovely thing it is. There's this poor devil, this corpse, you see, lying on the table with his guts laid open and all these students . . .'

'Do you mind,' said Wexford. 'I'm just going to have my lunch. You doctors bring your revolting trade into everything. We can hear your ideas on interior decoration another time. Now I want to know about Charlie Hatton.'

'Perfectly healthy bloke,' said the doctor, 'bar the fact that he's dead.' He ignored Burden's glance of reproof. 'Someone bashed him on the back on the head with a heavy smooth object. I'd say he was dead by eleven but it's impossible to be accurate about these things. What did you say he did for a living?'

'He was a lorry driver,' said Burden.

'I thought that's what you said. He'd got a marvellous set of teeth.'

'So what?' said Wexford. 'He ought to have had good teeth.' Rather ruefully he ran his tongue over the two stumps that held in place his upper plate. 'He was only thirty.'

'Sure,' said Crocker, 'he ought to have had his own being a war baby and a cog in the welfare state. The point is he didn't. What I meant was he'd got just about the finest set of *false* teeth I've ever seen. Lovely ivory castles. Very nifty grinders Charlie Hatton had, all cunningly contrived to look more real than the real thing. I'd be surprised if they cost less than two hundred quid.'

'Rich man,' said Wexford ruminatively. 'A hundred pounds in his wallet and two hundred in his mouth. I wish I could believe he'd come by it honestly, driving his lorry up and down the Great North Road.'

'That's your problem,' said the doctor. 'Well, I'm away to my lunch. Tried the lift yet?'

'In your capacity as my medical adviser, you advised me to walk upstairs. Physician, heal thyself. About all the exercise you get is pressing the button on your automatic gear change. You want to watch your blood pressure, too.'

'I should worry,' said Crocker. He went to the door where the sunshine showed off his elegant figure and absence of paunch to best advantage. 'All a matter of metabolism,' he said airily. 'Some have it rapid.' He looked back at Wexford. 'Others slow. The luck of the draw.'

Wexford gave a snort. When the doctor had gone, he opened the top drawer of his desk and took from it the contents of Charlie Hatton's pockets. The wallet was there, but it was empty of money. It was still soaking wet and now Wexford carefully removed from its leather partitions a photograph of Lilian Hatton, a driving licence and a darts club membership card and spread them in the sun to dry.

In the pocket also there had been a clean handkerchief with a small card caught between its folds. You couldn't see the card until you unfolded the handkerchief and now Wexford looked at it for the first time. It too was wet and the ink writing on it indecipherable, but it was still recognisable as the pasteboard square dentists use to remind patients of their appointments. On the top was printed: *Jolyon Vigo, B.D.S., L.D.S., R.C.S., Eng., Dent. Surg., 19 Ploughman's Lane, Kingsmarkham, Sussex. Tel: Kingsmarkham 384.*

Wexford held it up in the bright shaft of sunlight.

'The source of the delectable dentures, d'you reckon?'

'Maybe Vigo can tell us where the money came from if Cullam can't,' said Burden. 'My wife goes to Vigo. He's a good dentist.'

'A fly one too, if you ask me, getting a sharp little customer like Charlie Hatton to part with two hundred for thirty-two teeth. No wonder he can afford to live in Ploughman's Lane. We're in the wrong job here, Mike, and no mistake. I'm going for my lunch now. Join me? And then we'll go and root Cullam out of his domestic bliss.'

'May as well use the lift,' said Burden with a trace of self-consciousness.

It was more than Wexford's life was worth to admit his craven fear of the lift. Although a notice clearly stated its capacity to carry three persons, he was secretly afraid that it would be inadequate to bear his vast bulk. But he hesitated for no more than a moment before stepping inside and when the door was closed he took refuge in clowning.

'Soft furnishings, table linen, cutlery,' he said facetiously, pressing the button. The lift sighed and began to sink. 'First floor for ladies' underwear, stockings . . . Why's it stopping, Mike?'

'Maybe you pressed the wrong button.'

Or it won't stand my weight, Wexford thought, alarmed. The lift came to rest at the first floor and the door slid open. Sergeant Camb hesitated apologetically on the threshold.

'Sorry, sir. I didn't know it was you. I can walk down.'

'*Three* persons are permitted, Sergeant,' Wexford said, hoping his now very real trepidation didn't show. 'Come along.'

'Thank you, sir.'

'Not bad, is it? The tribute of a grateful government.' Come on, come on, he thought, and pictured the three of them plummeting down the last thirty feet into the basement.

'You off to see Mrs. Fanshawe, I suppose?' he said superfluously. The lift floated lightly, steadied and the door opened. Must be stoutly built, thought Wexford, like me. 'I heard she'd regained consciousness.'

'I'm hoping the doctors'll have broken the news about her husband and her daughter, sir,' said Camb as they crossed the black and white checkerboard foyer of the station. 'It's not a job I fancy. They were all the family she'd got. She hasn't a soul in the world barring her sister who came down and identified the bodies.'

'How old is she?'

'Mrs. Fanshawe, sir? Fifty odd. The sister's a good bit older. Horrible business for her having to identify Miss Fanshawe. She was a nasty mess, I can tell you. Face all . . .'

'I'm just off for my lunch,' said Wexford firmly.

He marched through the swing doors in front of the others and Camb got into his car. The stone flowerpots on the forecourt sported bright pink bouquets of *pelargoniums*, their magenta-splashed faces turned gratefully to the noonday sun.

'What was that all about?' asked Burden.

'Mrs. Fanshawe? It's not our cup of tea. She and her husband were driving home from Eastbourne in Fanshawe's Jaguar. It overturned in the fast lane on the twin-track road on the other side of Stowerton. Their home was in London and Fanshawe must have been in a hurry. God knows how it happened, there wasn't another thing on the road, but the Jag overturned and caught fire. Mrs. Fanshawe was flung clear, the other two killed outright. Badly burned too.'

'And this Mrs. Fanshawe doesn't know?'

'She's been in a coma since it happened six weeks ago.'

'I remember now,' said Burden, lifting the plastic strip curtain the Carousel Café hung up in hot weather to keep out wasps. 'The inquest was adjourned.'

'Till Mrs. F. regained consciousness. Presumably Camb's going to try and get her to tell him just why a seasoned driver like Fanshawe overturned his car on an empty road. Some hopes! What d'you fancy for lunch, Mike? I'm going for the salad myself.'

'Two ham salads,' said Burden to the waitress. He poured himself some water from a chilled carafe.

'Getting quite transatlantic the old Carousel,' said Wexford. 'And about time too. Not so long ago the water used to steam away like a perishing engine on these tables in hot weather. What's the betting this McCloy's running a big racket, paying Charlie Hatton to leave his lorry unattended and paying him to keep other lorry drivers occupied whenever the chance presents itself? Lorries are always getting hi-jacked. They leave them in these lay-bys while they have a little kip or a cup of tea. Hatton could have done a nice little distracting job there. Fifty or a hundred quid a lorry depending on the load.'

'In that case, why does McCloy kill the goose that lays the golden eggs?'

'Because Hatton gets scared or fed-up and threatens to rat on him. He may even have tried blackmail.'

'I shouldn't be a bit surprised,' said Burden, spreading butter on his roll. The butter was almost liquid. Like the rest of humanity, he reflected, the Carousel staff were disappointingly inconsistent.

5

'BUT MY DAUGHTER wasn't in the car.'

Seldom had Sergeant Camb felt so sorry for anyone as he did for this woman who lay against the piled pillows. His heart ached for her. And yet she was in one of the nicest private rooms in the hospital; she had a telephone and a television; her nightgown was a silly frou-frou of frills and spilling lace and on her thin fingers the rings—diamonds and sapphires in platinum—rattled as she clasped and unclasped the sheet.

It's true what they say, money can't buy happiness, thought the simple sergeant. He had noticed there were no flowers in the room and only one 'get well' card on the table by the chair where the policewoman sat. From her sister, he supposed. She hadn't anyone else now, not a soul in the world. Her husband was dead and her daughter . . .

'I'm very very sorry, Mrs. Fanshawe,' he said, 'but your daughter *was* in the car. She was travelling back to London with you and your husband.'

'They didn't suffer,' put in the young policewoman quickly. 'They can't have felt a thing.'

Mrs. Fanshawe touched her forehead where the dyed hair showed half an inch of white at the roots. 'My head,' she said. 'My head aches. I can't remember things, not details. Everything's so vague.'

'Don't you worry,' said Camb heartily. 'You'll find you'll get your memory back in time. You're going to get quite well, you know.' For what? For widowhood, for childlessness?

'Your sister's been able to supply us with most of the details we need.'

They had been close, Mrs. Fanshawe and Mrs. Browne, and there wasn't much about the Fanshawes Mrs. Browne hadn't known. From her they had learned that Jerome Fanshawe had a bungalow at Eastover between Eastbourne and Seaford and that he and his wife and daughter had driven down there for a week's holiday on May 17th. The daughter Nora had left her post as an English teacher in a German school before Easter. She was between jobs, at a loose end, Camb had gathered, otherwise nothing would have induced her to accompany her parents. But she had accompanied them. Mrs. Browne had been at their Mayfair flat and seen them all off together.

They had left Eastover days earlier than had been expected. Mrs. Browne couldn't account for that, unless it had been because of the wet weather. Perhaps no one would ever know the reason, for Jerome Fanshawe's Jaguar had skidded, crashed and caught fire five miles from the hospital where the sole survivor now lay.

'I won't bother you for long,' Camb said gently. 'Perhaps you can't remember much about the crash. Do you think you could try and tell me what you do remember?'

Dorothy Fanshawe had forgotten who these kind though tiresome people were, just as she had again forgotten where she was. Her sister had been to see her and made her very tired and various strangers had moved her and pummelled her in a familiar manner that made her angry. Then someone had told her that Jerome was dead and had waited for her to cry. Mrs. Fanshawe had twisted her rings—they were a great comfort to her, those rings—and said:

'Then it's all mine now, mine and Nora's.'

They thought she was wandering and they went away. She was glad to see the back of them with their interfering ways and their lack of respect. There was only one person she wanted to see and that was why she stared so searchingly into the young pretty face of the policewoman. But she had been in a coma, she wasn't mad. She knew very well this wasn't the right face. 'Am I in London?' she asked clearly and briskly.

'No, Mrs. Fanshawe,' said the sergeant, thinking how quavering and weak her voice was. 'You're in Stowerton Royal Infirmary, Stowerton in Sussex.'

'You seem very well-informed,' said Mrs. Fanshawe, pleased because she had succeeded so well in pulling herself together. 'Perhaps you can tell me why my daughter doesn't come to see me? Haven't they told her I'm here? Nora would want to know. She'd come home.'

'Oh, Mrs. Fanshawe . . .' The policewoman sounded very wretched, almost distraught, and catching her eye, Sergeant Camb gave her a sharp reproving glance. Better leave it, the look said. Maybe it's more merciful this way. Let her learn about it by degrees. The mind has its own way of softening blows, he thought sententiously.

'Now back to the—er, accident,' he said. 'Just try and see if you can tell me what happened when you left Eastover. It was getting dark and there wasn't much traffic on the road, it being a Monday. It had been raining and the road was wet. Now, Mrs. Fanshawe?'

'My husband was driving,' she began and she wondered why the man's face wore such a sloppy expression. Perhaps he had noticed her rings. She slid them up and down her fingers, suddenly remembering that the five of them were worth nearly twenty thousand pounds. 'Jerome was driving . . .' What a silly name it was. Like *Three Men in a Boat*. That made her giggle, although the sound came out like a harsh crackle. 'I sat beside him, of course, and I was knitting. I must have been knitting. I always do when Jerome drives. He drives so fast,' she said querulously. 'Much too fast and he never takes any notice when I tell him to go slower, so I do my knitting. To keep my mind off it, you know.'

Mean and selfish Jerome was. A man of fifty-five hadn't any business to drive like a crazy teenager. She had told him that, but he had ignored her like he ignored everything else she ever said. Still, she was used to being ignored. Nora never took any notice of what she said either. When she came to think of it, the only thing she and Jerome had ever agreed about was what a difficult, trying and utterly maddening creature Nora was. It was exactly like her to go away and not get in touch with her parents. Jerome would have something to say about that . . . Then there swam pleasantly into her muddled mind the recollection that Jerome would never have anything to say about anything again, never drive at eighty-five or pick on Nora or do those other terrible and humiliating things. Tonight, when she felt better, she would write to Nora and tell her her father was dead. With Jerome out of the way and all that money for themselves, she felt they would have a much happier relationship . . .

'I was knitting a jumper for Nora,' she said. What a marvellous constitution she must have to remember that after all she'd been through! 'Not that she deserved it, the naughty girl.' Now, why had she said that? Nora had been naughty much naughtier than ever before, but for the life of her Dorothy Fanshawe couldn't remember of what that naughtiness had consisted. She wished the policeman or whoever he was would wipe that mawkish sheeplike expression off his face. There was no need for anyone to feel sorry for her, Dorothy Fanshawe, of Astbury Mews, Upper Grosvenor Street, W.1. She was a merry widow now, rich in her own right, soon to be well again, the mother of a good-looking talented only daughter. 'I don't remember what we talked about,' she said, 'my *late* husband and I. Nothing, probably. The road was wet and I kept telling him to go slower.'

'Your daughter was in the back seat, Mrs. Fanshawe?'

Oh! really, how absurd the man was! 'Nora was *not*

in the car. I keep telling you. Nora went back to Germany. No doubt she is in Germany now.'

To the sergeant the jerky bumbling words sounded like the raving of a madwoman. In spite of what the doctors said, it seemed to him probable that the accident had irremediably damaged her brain. He didn't dare take it upon himself to enlighten her further. God knew what harm he might do! Sooner or later, if she ever got her reason back, she would realise that her daughter had resigned from this German job six weeks before the accident, that she hadn't breathed a word to her aunt or her friends about the possibility of her returning to Europe. The girl's body had been identified by her aunt, Mrs. Browne. She was dead and buried.

'I expect she is,' he said soothingly. 'No doubt she is. What made your husband swerve, Mrs. Fanshawe?'

'I was knitting.'

'Did you hit something, did a tyre burst?'

'I told you, I didn't look. I was knitting.'

'Did your husband cry out, say anything?'

'I think he said "My God",' said Mrs. Fanshawe. She couldn't really remember anything, only that she had been knitting and then she had woken up in this bed with her nosy, bossy sister sitting beside her. But Jerome was always saying 'My God' or even 'My Christ'. He had a limited vocabulary and she had stopped telling him not to be blasphemous twenty years ago. 'I don't remember anything else,' she said. That was all they were going to get out of her. She wasn't going to waste her strength. She needed it for the letter she was going to write in a minute to Nora.

Camb looked compassionately at the quivering febrile mouth and the long unfiled nails that played with those rings. Mrs. Fanshawe had told him nothing. Perhaps he ought to have realised it was too soon, or his superiors ought to have realised. They would have to go now anyway. The young lady doctor had said ten minutes, but they must have been here twenty. Here was the nurse coming now. Funny uniforms they wear these days, he thought, eyeing the girl's navy-blue ny-

lon overall and hat like a white forage cap. Poor Mrs.
Fanshawe was staring at her desperately. No wonder,
exhausted and broken-hearted as she was.

No, it wasn't Nora. Just for a split second Mrs. Fanshawe had thought it was. But Nora never wore an
overall, she despised housework—and this girl was
wearing an overall, not the rather smart dress for which
Mrs. Fanshawe had first taken it. She had a cap on her
head too. Was it possible that her sister had taken on a
new maid for the Fanshawes' flat and not said anything
about it? More than possible, considering how interfering her sister was. Interfering but irresponsible. A re-
sponsible person would have sent for Nora by now.

'What's your name?' Mrs. Fanshawe said sharply.

'Rose, Mrs. Fanshawe. Nurse Rose. I've come to
make you more comfy and bring you your tea. You
could drink a nice cup of tea, couldn't you? I'm afraid
you'll have to run along now Sergeant. I can't allow my
patient any setbacks, you know.'

Very talkative, thought Mrs. Fanshawe. Takes a lot
upon herself. She tried to sit up.

'Rose,' she said. 'I want to write a letter to my
daughter, my daughter in Germany. Will you fetch me
writing paper and a pen, please?'

She doesn't know, Camb thought, she's new. Nobody's told her. Just as well. He intercepted the policewoman's glance and crushed it with a frown.

'We *are* getting better, aren't we?' said the nurse skit-
tishly. 'Writing letters! Well, I don't know, I'm sure.
I'm certain you haven't got any paper of your own. I'll
tell you what I'll do, I'll just pop down the corridor
and borrow some from Mrs. Goodwin in number four.
Then I'll post your letter when I go off duty, shall I?'

'That will be very kind of you,' said Mrs. Fanshawe
austerely. 'Then you can bring the tea.'

A pert girl and probably untrainable, she thought.
Time would show. At any rate, Jerome wouldn't be
there to upset this one, catch her in corners and smack
her bottom like he had the Danish *au pair*. Jerome was

dead. She'd always said he'd kill himself driving like that and now he had. Why hadn't he killed her too? What good fortune had decreed that she be saved and be sitting here in her own bed in her own flat?

But it wasn't her own bed and her own flat. Very carefully Mrs. Fanshawe marshalled her thoughts and her memories. Jerome was dead. Nora was in Germany and she was in Something-or-other Royal Infirmary. A hospital. Very thoughtful of someone to have engaged a maid for her in hospital.

Unless this Rose was a nurse. Of course, she must be a nurse. What a fool I am, thought Mrs. Fanshawe. I feel exactly as if I were having a very prolonged dream but every time I come out of it I'm so tired I fall back into it again.

The inaccurate information given by all these busybodies didn't help at all. People were so inefficient these days. First her sister had forgotten to inform Nora, then this policeman said Nora had been with her and Jerome in the Jaguar. They must all think she was out of her mind. As if a mother didn't know where her own daughter was! Why she even remembered Nora's address.

Goethestrasse 14, Köln, West Germany. Mrs. Fanshawe was very proud of the way she wrote Köln like that instead of Cologne. What reserves of strength and intellect she must have to remember details like that! And after all she'd been through. Presently the nurse came back with the paper.

'Thank you, Nurse,' said Mrs. Fanshawe to show what a fine grasp of things she had. She tried to hold the pen, but it zig-zagged all over the paper like that Planchette thing her father had used long ago.

'Why not let me write it for you?' said Nurse Rose.

'Perhaps it would be better. I'll dictate. Shall I begin?'

Nurse Rose had to exercise all her powers of concentration to sort out from the mumblings and digressions exactly what Mrs. Fanshawe wanted to say. But she was a kind-hearted girl and, besides, it always paid to be attentive to patients in the private wing. Last year when one of them had left after only a fortnight she had given Nurse Rose a travelling clock and a nearly full bottle of *Rochas' Femme*.

' "Dearest Nora," ' she read aloud, ' "I am almost well again and think you should come and see me. Poor Daddy would have wished it. I expect auntie has told you everything and you have been too busy to come, but please come now. We will let bygones be bygones. Love from Mummy." That all right, Mrs. Fanshawe? I've got some stamps, enough to make up to ninepence. I think I'll pop it in the post now when I go for my tea.'

Coming back from the pillar box at the end of Charteris Road, Nurse Rose met the Private Wing sister.

'I've just been posting a letter for poor Mrs. Fanshawe, Sister,' she said virtuously. 'I like to do what I can, you know. Anything to cheer them up. She was so keen to get a letter to her daughter off tonight.'

'Her daughter's dead.'

'Oh, Sister, you don't mean it! Oh God, how dreadful! I never dreamt, I never guessed . . . Ooh, Sister!'

'You'd better get back on duty, Nurse, and do try not to be so impulsive.'

6
===

THE CHILD WHO opened the door to him was the one that had been out in the fields with his father. He was a boy of about seven, big for his age, aggressive looking and with food adhering to his face in greasy red and brown streaks.

'Who is it, Dominic?' came a voice from the sleazy

depths of this small and totally inadequate council house.

'A man,' said Dominic simply.

'What does he want?'

To put an end to all this pointless colloquy, Wexford stepped into the hall, then the living room. Three more children were watching athletics on television. The remains of lunch were still on the stained crumb-scattered tablecloth and a woman sat at the table feeding a baby from a bottle. She might have been any age between thirty and sixty and Wexford set the lower limit so low only because of her young children. Her hair was thin and fair and long, caught back with an elastic band, and her face was thin and long too, wizened and pinched. A weariness that was as much chronic boredom as physical tiredness seemed the most dominant thing about her. It was the sordid exhaustion of poverty, of overwork, of perpetual near-incarceration, of eternal nagging demands, and to be left alone just to sit for perhaps only five minutes in unthinking apathy was her sole remaining desire. To this end she never wasted a word or a gesture and when she saw Wexford she neither greeted him nor even lifted her head, but said to one of her little girls:

'Go and fetch your dad, Samantha.'

Samantha jerked a thick black cat off her lap and trailed listlessly via the kitchen to the back garden. A middle-class woman, a woman with more money and fewer children, might have apologised for the squalor and the smell of a hundred stale meals. Mrs. Cullam didn't even look at him and when he asked her at what time her husband had come home on Friday night she said laconically, 'Quarter past eleven.'

'How can you be so sure of the time?'

'It was a quarter past eleven.' Mrs. Cullam put the baby on the table among the crumbs, removing its napkin which she dropped on the floor, and said in the same low economical tone, 'Get me another nappie, Georgina.' A strong smell of ammonia fought with the cabbage. The baby, which was female, began to cry.

Mrs. Cullam lit a cigarette and stood against the table, her hands hanging by her sides, the cigarette dangling from her mouth. Georgina came back with a grey rag, sat down and watched her brother poke his fingers in the cat's ears. 'Leave the cat alone, Barnabas,' said Mrs. Cullam.

Her husband came in, drying his hands on a tea cloth, the black dog cowering at his heels. He nodded to Wexford and then he turned off the television.

'Get up, Samantha, and let the gentleman sit down.' The child took no notice and made no sound when her father slapped one arm and yanked her up by the other. He viewed the room helplessly, paying particular attention to the discarded napkin, but there was no disgust on his face, only a vaguely resentful acceptance.

Wexford didn't take the vacant seat and something in his expression must have told Cullam he wanted privacy, for he said to his wife, 'Can't you get them kids out of here?'

Mrs. Cullam shrugged and the ash from her cigarette fell into a plate of congealing gravy. She hoisted the baby on to her hip and dragging a chair close up to the television set, sat down and stared at the blank screen. 'Leave the cat alone, I said,' she remarked without heat.

'What were you wanting?' Cullam asked.

'We'll go into your kitchen, if you don't mind, Mr. Cullam.'

'It's in a right old mess.'

'Never mind.'

Mrs. Cullam made no comment. She switched on the television without looking up. Two of the children began to fight in the depths of their armchair. Wexford followed their father into the kitchen. There was nowhere to sit so, pushing aside the handles of four encrusted saucepans, he leant against the gas cooker.

'I only want to know who McCloy is,' he said mildly.

Cullam gave him a look of not altogether comfortable cunning. 'How d'you know about McCloy, anyway?'

'Come on now, you know I can't tell you that.' The children were screaming now above the sound of the racy athletics commentary. Wexford closed the door and he heard Mrs. Cullam say, 'Leave the bleeding cat alone, Barnabas.' She had wasted a word. 'You know who he is,' Wexford said. 'Now you can tell me.'

'I don't know. Honest I don't.'

'You don't know who he is, but last night in the pub you asked Mr. Hatton if he'd been seeing much of McCloy lately. You wouldn't touch McCloy because you like to sleep quiet in your bed.'

'I tell you, I don't know who he is and I never saw him.'

Wexford removed his elbow from its dangerous proximity to a half-full plate of cold chips. 'You didn't like Mr. Hatton very much, did you? You wouldn't walk home with him, though he was going your way. So you went on ahead and maybe you hung about a bit under those trees.' Pursuing the line, he watched Cullam's big beefy face begin to lose colour. 'I reckon you must have done, Cullam. A strong young fellow like you doesn't take thirty-five minutes to get here from the Kingsbrook bridge.'

In a low, resentful voice, Cullam said, 'I was sick. I was nearly home and I come over queer. I'm not used to scotch and I went into the gents down by the station to be sick.'

'Let me congratulate you on your powers of recovery. You were fit enough to be out on a country walk at seven-thirty this morning. Or were you just popping back to see you'd left Hatton neat and tidy? I want to see the clothes you wore last night.'

'They're out on the line.'

Wexford looked at him, his eyebrows almost vanishing into the vestiges of his hair, and the implications in that look were unmistakable. Cullam fidgeted, he moved to the crock-filled sink, leaning on it compressing his lips.

'I washed them,' he said. 'Pullover and trousers and a shirt. They was—well, they were in a bit of a state.' He shifted his feet.

'Charming,' Wexford said unkindly. '*You* washed them? What d'you have a wife for?' For the first time he noticed the washing machine, a big gleaming automatic affair, and the only object in that kitchen that was not stained or chipped or coated with clotted food drips. He opened the back door and eyed the sagging clothesline from which the three garments Cullam had named hung between a row of napkins. 'The blessings of modern mechanisation,' he said. 'Very nice too. I often remark these days how the roles of the sexes have been reversed.' His voice became deceptively friendly and Cullam licked his thick lips. 'A man can be dead tired after a week's work but he can still give his wife a helping hand. One touch of a button and the family wash comes out whiter than white. In fact, a gadget like that turns chores into pleasure, you might say. Men are all little boys at heart, when all's said and done, and it's not only women that like to have these little playthings about to make a break in the daily round. Besides, they cost so much, you might as well get some fun out of them. Don't tell me that little toy cost you less than a hundred and twenty, Cullam.'

'A hundred and twenty-five,' said Cullam with modest pride. He was quite disarmed and, advancing upon the machine, he opened the gleaming porthole. 'You set your programme . . . .' A last uneasy look at the chief inspector told him his visitor was genuinely interested, paying no more than a routine call. 'Put in your powder,' he said, 'and Bob's your uncle.'

'I knew a fellow,' Wexford lied ruminatively, 'a lorry driver like yourself. Big family too and we all know what inroads a big family makes. He got in bad company, I'm sorry to say. His wife kept on at him, you see, wanting more gear about the house. He'd already turned a blind eye when a couple of his lorries got hijacked. Well, you can't call it a crime, can you, looking the other way in a café when somebody's nicking your vehicle from a lay-by?' Cullam closed the porthole, keeping his head turned. 'They paid well, this bad company. Mind you, this fellow jibbed a bit when they offered him two hundred to knock off a bloke who wouldn't play along with them, but not for long. He reckoned he'd a right to nice things the same as this bad company he'd got in with. And why not? We're all equal these days. Share and share alike, this fellow said. So he hung about in a lonely spot one night, just where the other fellow was due to pass by and—well, Bob's your uncle, as you so succinctly put it. He's doing twelve years, as a matter of fact.'

Cullam looked at him, truculently disillusioned.

'I saved up my overtime for that washer,' he said.

'Sure it wasn't McCloy's little dropsy for services rendered? Isn't a man's life worth a hundred and twenty nicker, Cullam? There's a sump on that machine of yours, you know. I can't help asking myself if there's blood and hair and brains in that sump, you know. Oh, you needn't look like that. We could find it. We can take that machine apart this afternoon, and your drains. They're a funny council, Sewingbury. I knew a family—six children in that case there were—they got evicted neck and crop just because they cracked a drainpipe. Vandalism, the council called it. We'll get your drains up, Cullam, but we're busy right now. I don't reckon we could find the labour to get them put back again.'

'You bastard,' said Cullam.

'I didn't hear that. My hearing's not what it was, but I haven't got one foot in the grave. I'd like to sit down, though. You can take that rubbish off that chair and wipe it, will you?'

Cullam sat on his washing machine, his long legs dangling. Behind the closed door the programme had changed from athletics to wrestling and once more the baby had begun to cry.

'I told you,' said its father, 'I don't know who McCloy is and I don't. I just said that to Charlie to needle him. Always bragging and boasting, he got on my wick.'

Wexford didn't have to absorb any more of the squalor to see what Cullam meant. This house was the very embodiment of sleazy noisy discomfort. It was a discomfort which would have brief pause only while its inhabitants slept and it extended from the top to the lowest level. The man and his wife were weighed down by almost every burden known to the philoprogenitive, ill-paid artisan; their children were miserable, badly brought up and perhaps ill-treated; their home over-crowded, even their animals wretchedly tormented. The parents had neither the character nor the love to make coping and organisation tenable. He remembered Charlie Hatton's brand-new flat, the pretty young wife with her smart clothes. These two men did the same sort of job. Or did they?

'If I tell you how it was,' Cullam said, 'you won't believe me.'

'Maybe not, try me.'

Cullam put his elbows on his knees and leant forward.

'It was in a café,' he said. 'One of them places where they have rooms for drivers to kip down for the night. Up on the A.1 between Stamford and Grantham. I was coming up to my eleven hours—we're not supposed to drive for more than eleven hours—and I went in and there was Charlie Hatton. I'd seen his lorry in the lay-by. We had a bite to eat and got talking.'

'What load do you carry?'

'Tyres, rubber tyres. While we was having our meal I looked out of the window and there was a fellow there—in the lay-by—sitting in a black car. I don't know why, but I didn't much like the look of him. I said so to Charlie, but all he said was I was like an old woman. He was always saying that to folks. Then he got me and two more drivers to go into his room for a hand of pontoon. He said it was quieter in there, but I couldn't see the lay-by from his room and after a bit I went outside. The fellow in the car was still there.'

'Did you take the number? Could you describe him?'

'I don't know.' Cullam gave him a shifty look. 'I never took the number. I sat in the cab for half an hour and then this fellow went off. Charlie'd said he wanted to phone Lilian and when I come back over the road he was in a phone box. I wanted a light for my fag—I'd run out of matches—so I opened the door of the box and just asked Charlie for a light. Well, I don't reckon he'd heard me coming. "Tell Mr. McCloy it's no dice," I heard him say and it was then I said had he got a match? He jumped out of his skin like he'd been stung. "What the hell are you up to," he shouts at me, "interfering with my private phone calls?" He was as white as a sheet.'

'You connected this call with the man in the car?'

'I reckon I did,' Cullam said, 'I did afterwards when I thought about it. My mind went back a couple of months to when Charlie'd asked me if I'd like to make a bit on the side. I wasn't interested and that was all there was. But I never forgot the name McCloy and when Charlie got so cocky in the pub I thought I'd needle him a bit. That's all.'

'When was the café incident, Cullam?'

'Come again?'

'When did you overhear Hatton's phone conversation?'

'Way back in the winter. January, I reckon. Not long after Charlie had his lorry pinched and got hit on the head.'

'All right. That'll do for now, but I may want to talk to you again.'

Wexford went back through the Cullams' living room. The children had disappeared. Mrs. Cullam still sat in front of the television, the baby asleep now in her lap, the dog lying across her slippered feet. She moved her head as he crossed the room and for a moment he thought she was going to speak to him. Then he saw that the movement was a mere craning of the neck because for an instant he had obstructed her view of the screen.

Dominic, Barnabas, Samantha and Georgina were sitting on the kerb poking sticks through the drain cover. Wexford wasn't inclined to be sentimental over the Cullams but he couldn't help being faintly touched that they who were poor in everything had been affluent, extravagant and imaginative in one respect. If they never gave their children another thing, they had at least endowed them with names usually reserved to the upper classes.

Dominic, whose face was still coated with food, looked up truculently as he passed and Wexford said, because he couldn't resist it:

'What's the baby called?'

'Jane,' said Dominic simply and without surprise.

When Wexford got home for his tea Clytemnestra wagged her darning-wool tail at him but she didn't get out of his chair. Wexford scowled at her.

'Where's Sheila?' he asked his wife.

'Dentist's.'

'She never said anything about toothache.'

'You don't go to the dentist's because you've got toothache any more. You go for a check-up. She's having that molar of hers crowned.'

'So I suppose she won't feel up to taking that creature out in the morning. Well, she needn't put it on to me. I've got enough on my plate.'

But Sheila danced in gaily at six o'clock and smiled at her father to show off the triumph of orthodontics.

'There, isn't that great?' To satisfy her Wexford peered into the perfect mouth. 'That filling was getting a bit of a drag,' she said. 'Very shy-making for close-ups. An actress has to think about these things.'

'I bet Bernhardt never bothered about her teeth,' said Wexford to annoy her.

Sheila opened her eyes wide and fixed her father with a precisely constructed look of wistful adoration. 'Did you often see Bernhardt when you were a young man, Pop?' she asked.

Wexford's reply was an ill-tempered snort. He

pushed a cup of tea to his daughter who rejected it in favour of cold milk. This she sipped slowly, very conscious of the picture she made in her cream linen dress, her pale hair slightly but attractively disordered, Roman sandal thongs binding her long legs to the knee. Wexford wondered what life held for her. Would she succeed and the future be a succession of triumphs, starring parts, world tours, fame, the increasing terror of growing old? Or would she marry some young idiot like this Sebastian and forget all her aspirations in the possession of two children and a semi? Because he was a father and no longer young he confessed to himself that he would prefer the latter. He wanted her to be safe. Nothing on earth would have made him tell her so.

No such thoughts troubled her, he fancied. Living in the moment, she drank her milk and began to prattle on about her visit to the dentist.

'If I ever settle down . . .' Sheila said this in much the same tone of incredulity as she might have said, 'If I ever die.' 'If I ever settle down, I wouldn't mind a house like his. Not in Kingsmarkham of course. Stratford might be nice or the Cotswolds near Stratford.'

'Within commuting distance,' Wexford put in slyly.

His daughter ignored him. 'One of those black and white houses it is. Terribly ancient and full of atmosphere. Of course, the surgery part's all modern. New copies of *Nova* and *Elle*. I thought that progressive.'

'Thoughtful too,' said Wexford, 'what with everyone in Kingsmarkham being bi-lingual.'

'Your generation just wasn't educated, Pop, but I can tell you I hardly know *anyone* who doesn't read French. Anyway, the old fuddy-duddies can look at the antiques.' Sheila put her glass down and tossed her head. 'Georgeous painting on the walls, and some marvellous glass sculpture.'

Sounds like the police station, Wexford thought. 'And where is this shrine of culture?' he said aloud.

'Ploughman's Lane.'

'He wouldn't be called Vigo would he?'

'Mm-hm, he would.' Sheila sat on the sofa and began painting shiny black lines on her eyelids. 'It's about time you and Mummy stopped going to that dreary old Richardson in the High Street and switched to Mr. Vigo.' The most difficult feat of her artistry completed, she started to stroke her lashes with a mascara wand. 'Mr. Vigo is an absolute dream. One of those fair-haired characters with a craggy face. Madly sexy.' Wexford winced and hoped she hadn't seen. His daughters were still little girls to him. Who the hell did this craggy fair fellow think he was, projecting his dreamy sexiness at his little girl? 'Of course he's not *young*,' said Sheila serenely.

'All of thirty-five, I daresay. One foot in the grave and the other on a bar of soap.'

'About thirty-five,' said Sheila seriously. She held her eyelashes up with two fingers to curl them. 'He's got a baby of six months and—something rather tragic. His older child's a mongol. Ghastly, isn't it? It's eight now and Mr. Vigo hasn't seen it for years. He and his wife tried and tried to have another one and they did, but it took them all those years. Of course he worships the baby.'

'How do you know all this?' Wexford asked. She was a detective's daughter all right. 'I thought you went to get your tooth done, not do a survey.'

'Oh, we had a long talk,' Sheila said airily. 'I don't suppose you can understand, but I'm interested in human nature. If I'm going to be a real actress I'll have to know what makes people tick. I'm getting quite good at summing people up.'

'Bully for you,' said her father sourly. 'I've been trying for forty years and the margin of error's still about eighty per cent.'

Sheila looked at herself in her handbag mirror. 'Mr. Vigo's got a very smooth sophisticated manner. Cool, if you know what I mean. I sometimes think dentists have a very interesting relationship with their patients. They've got to be nice, have the right psychological approach, otherwise you'd never go back to them again, would you? It's such an intimate thing. I mean, can you think of any other situation, Pop, when a man gets so close to a woman except when he's actually making love to her?'

'I sincerely hope nothing like that happened.'

'Oh, Pop . . . I was just saying what it was *like*. I was making a sort of comparison.' Sheila giggled and twisted a strand of hair around one finger. 'Although, when I was going he did give me a sort of squeeze and said I'd got the loveliest mouth he'd ever seen.'

'My God!' said Wexford, getting up. 'If you don't mind what you say to your father, you might remember he's also a detective chief inspector.' He paused and then said, not realising the effect his words would have, 'I may go along and see this Vigo.'

'Oh, Pop!' Sheila wailed.

'Not because of your lovely mouth, my dear. In pursuance of an enquiry of my own.'

'Well, don't you dare . . .'

All this time Mrs. Wexford had been placidly eating ginger biscuits, but now she looked up and said calmly:

'What a silly girl you are. I often think it's a blessing intelligence isn't necessary in the interpretive arts. If you've finished with your face you'd better take that dog out.'

At the word dog, Clytemnestra uncurled herself.

'All right,' said Sheila meekly.

7

THEY STOOD UNDER the willow trees, looking at the river. Anyone who didn't know them might have taken them for a couple of businessmen out for a Sunday afternoon stroll.

But almost everyone in Kingsmarkham knew them and knew also by now that this was the spot where Charlie Hatton had been murdered.

'I said we'd have to talk to everyone in the darts club,' said Burden, stopping down at the water's edge, 'and I reckon we have. Funny, isn't it? Pertwee's the only one who could put up with Hatton for a moment, but no one's willing to come out with it. It's always the others who were daggers drawn with him. The one you're talking to is all tolerance and forbearance. The farthest he'll go is to admit a sort of resentment. Does a man do murder because a mate of his riles him in a pub or because he's got more money than he has?'

'He might if he was going to get some of the money,' said Wexford. 'A hundred pounds is a lot to a man like Cullam. We're going to have to watch Cullam, see if he does some big spending in the next few days. I'm not at all happy about the way he washed the clothes he was wearing on Friday night.'

Burden was advancing gingerly across the river, trying not to get his feet wet. He trod on the projecting stones which the water lapped without covering. Then he bent down and said, 'There's your weapon.'

From the bank Wexford followed the direction of his pointing finger. All but one of the stones were furred at their perimeters and partly on their surfaces with green weed. Burden was pointing to the only one that looked bare, as if until very recently it had lain with its exposed area embedded in the river's gravelly floor. He squatted precariously and lifted the stone in both hands. Then he eased himself to his feet and scrambled back to Wexford.

It was a big stone, not round, but elongated and shaped rather like a mandolin. The side which had lain on the river bed was green and moss-grown and there was nothing about it except for its shape and its anomalous position in the water to show that it might have been used as a lethal weapon. Wexford grasped it in both his hands, raised it high and brought it down hard to meet the empty air. Hatton had been walking along in the dark and someone had waited for him among the willows and the brambles, the stone ready for use. Full of whisky, his thoughts fuddled and far away, Hatton had given warning of his approach. He had been whistling and probably not bothering to tread softly. The stone had been raised high just as Wexford was raising it now but brought down that time on the back of Hatton's skull. Once, twice, more than that? As many times as it took to kill. Then Hatton had rolled into the water. His killer had rifled his wallet before casting the stone into the stream.

Wexford thought all these things and he knew Burden was following his thoughts, matching them, so he didn't bother to say anything. He dropped the stone and it rolled a little before falling into the water with a soft plop.

Across the meadows he could see the flats of the council estate, the sun striking their plate-glass windows and making them blaze as if the whole place was on fire.

'Since we've come so far,' he said, 'we may as well have another chat with Mrs. Hatton.'

Her mother was with her and three other people. Jack Pertwee sat on the smart checked tweed sofa holding the hand of a girl with a monumental pile of black hair and eyelashes like shoe brushes. Mrs. Hatton and her mother were both in black, smart unseasonable black relieved with a great deal of showy costume jewellery. The widow's suit looked brand-new and Wexford couldn't help wondering if she had actually been out the previous afternoon to buy it. She wore a white blouse with an ostentatious frilly jabot and a big paste spray on one lapel. Her stockings were dark and her shoes, though also apparently new, the outdated stiletto-heeled pointed kind of gleaming black patent. She looked as if she were about to set off for a provincial cocktail party, an office party of female executives.

At first Wexford felt a curious distaste and then he thought about the dead man and what he knew of him.

This was the way Charlie Hatton would have liked his widow to look, brave, defiant, bedizened. The last thing a cocky little man like Hatton would want was a kind of spiritual suttee.

He surveyed the rest of the company. Plainly they had interrupted a mourning tea party. The girl on the sofa must be the bride whose nuptials Hatton's death had deferred. And the other man?

'My brother, Mr. Bardsley,' said Mrs. Hatton. 'Him and Mum came to keep me company. This gentleman is Mr. Pertwee.'

'We've met,' said Wexford graciously.

'And Miss Thompson,' said Mrs. Hatton. She spoke in a low dutiful voice. Her eyes were swollen under the thick green and black make-up. 'They were all very fond of Charlie. Would you like a cup of tea? You can if you want. You're welcome.'

'We won't, thanks, Mrs. Hatton.'

'Well, sit down then, there's plenty of room.' She said it proudly, indicating the several empty chairs. They were good chairs, upholstered and cared for, not the uncomfortable dining seats with hard backs a less affluent hostess would be obliged to offer latecomers. Looking at the branched hanging lamp of teak and smoky glass, the velvet curtains and the big colour television set, Wexford decided that Hatton had done his wife proud. Cullam and he were both lorry drivers, both lived in council accommodation, but that was all they had in common. He glanced at Bardsley, the brother, a fair rabbity man, like his sister but less well-favoured, and he observed his suit. It was very likely his best suit—today of all days he would surely wear his best suit—but it was a cheap off-the-peg affair.

'Please forgive me, Mrs. Hatton, if I ask a few routine questions,' he said. She gave him a pleased earnest nod. 'You and Mr. Hatton were in business together, I understand, Mr. Bardsley?'

'That's right.'

'Was it a full partnership?'

Bardsley put his teacup down and said in a melancholy voice, 'I was thinking of taking him into partnership, but business hasn't been that good lately. As it was, he just worked for me.'

'Would you mind telling me what wages you paid him?'

'Well, I don't know . . . I don't rightly like to.'

'Of course he don't,' Jack Pertwee suddenly interrupted belligerently. 'What's it got to do with what happened on Friday?'

'That's right, Jack,' murmured the girl and she squeezed his hand.

'You can see Charlie did all right for himself. You've only got to look around you.'

'Don't make trouble, Jack,' Mrs. Hatton said with that peculiar intense control of hers. 'The officers are only doing what they have to.' She fingered her brooch uneasily. 'Charlie usually brought home a bit over twenty pounds a week. That's right, isn't it, Jim?'

Jim Bardsley looked unhappy about it and his voice became aggressive. 'I've been lucky to make that much myself lately,' he said. 'Charlie was one of the sort that make a little go a long way. I reckon he was careful.'

Marilyn Thompson tossed her head and a lock of hair drifted from the elaborate structure. 'He wasn't mean, anyway,' she flared, 'if that's what you mean by careful. There's not many men who aren't even relations that'd give someone a record player for a wedding present.'

'I never said he was mean, Marilyn.'

'It makes me sick. What you want to do is find who killed him.' The girl's hands trembled and she clenched them. 'Give us a cig, Jack.' Her hands enclosed Pertwee's wrist as he held the lighter and they were no more steady than his. 'You lot,' she muttered, 'you lot don't reckon nothing to a working man. If he hasn't got a nice home you call him a layabout.' She glared at Wexford, pushing back her hair. 'And if he's got things like your class take for granted you jump right on him, say he must have nicked them. Class, class, class,' she said, tears trembling on the brush-bristle lashes. 'That's all you think about.'

'Wait till the revolution comes,' said Bardsley nastily.

'Oh, shut up, the pair of you,' Mrs. Hatton said shrilly. She turned to Wexford, her controlled dignity returning. 'My husband did overtime,' she said, 'and he had his side lines.'

Side lines, Wexford thought. He got a little overtime and he made it go a long way. The man had colour television, false teeth worth two hundred pounds; he gave his friend a record player for a wedding present. Wexford had seen that glass and teak lamp in a Kingsmarkham shop and noted it had been priced at twenty-five pounds, one and a quarter times Hatton's weekly wage. When he was killed he had had a hundred pounds on him.

'If he's got things like your class take for granted,' the girl had said, 'you say he must have nicked them.' Curious, really, Wexford reflected, watching her huddled now in the crook of Pertwee's arm. Of course she was very young, probably got a Communist shop steward for a father, and doubtless went about sneering at people better-educated and better-spoken than herself. It was an aggressive type that had even reached Kingsmarkham, a type that talked pacifism and the rights of man and brotherly love without the energy or courage to do anything that might bring these desirable conditions nearer.

And yet he said nothing to provoke her outburst. Neither for that matter had Bardsley beyond hinting that Hatton had been prudent. Had she risen to this intangible slight bait because she knew Hatton's wealth had been dishonestly come by? If she knew it, green and uncouth as she was, Pertwee would know it also. Everyone in this room but Burden and himself might know it. Not for the first time he reflected on the power of grief. It is the perfect unassailable defence. Pertwee had already employed it the previous morning effectively to terminate interrogation. Mrs. Hatton, even more expertly, kept it under a piteous control that only a brute would have the brashness to disregard. She was moving about the room now, balancing painfully but stoically on her high heels, taking empty cups and plates from each of her guests with a gentle murmur for every one of them. Wexford took in the looks that passed to her from each of her visitors, her mother's merely solicitous, Pertwee's indicative of deep affection, Bardsley's shifty, while the thwarted bride leaned forward, stuck out her chin and nodded her utter committed partisanship.

'Did your husband have a bank account, Mrs. Hatton?' Burden asked as she passed his chair.

The sun was full on her face, showing every stroke and grain of make-up, but at the same time driving expression from it. She nodded, 'At the Midland,' she said.

'I'd like to see his paying-in book.'

'What for?'

The truculent harsh voice was Pertwee's. Wexford ignored him and followed the widow to the sideboard from a drawer of which she took a long cream-coloured book. He handed it to Burden and said, apparently inconsequentially:

'When did your husband get his false teeth, Mrs. Hatton?'

Pertwee's muttered 'Bloody nosy-parker' made her flinch a little and throw a desperate glance over her shoulder. 'He'd always had them. Had them since he was twenty' she said.

'This present set?'

'Oh, no. They were new. He went to Mr. Vigo for them about a month back.'

Nodding, Wexford eyed the paying-in book over Burden's shoulder and what he saw astonished him far more than any of Hatton's prodigality. Some three-quarters of all the slips in the book had been torn out and with the exception of three, all the stubs had been torn too.

On the most recent remaining stub the date was

April and on that occasion Hatton had paid into his
bank account the modest sum of five and fourpence.

'Fourth dividend on the pools that was,' Mrs. Hatton
said with a miserable gulp.

The other two stubs were filled in each with amounts
of two pounds.

'Mrs. Hatton,' he said, beckoning her into a corner.
'The purpose of these stubs in a paying-in book is for
the holder to have a record of the amount of money he
has deposited in his bank. Can you suggest to me why
Mr. Hatton tore them out? They must have been filled
in at the bank either by Mr. Hatton himself or else by
the cashier who was attending to him.'

'It's a mystery to me. Charlie never talked about
money to me. He always said . . .' She gulped again
and a tear trickled through the make-up. 'He always
said, "Don't worry your head about that. When we got
married I promised I'd give you everything you want
and so I will. You name it, you can have it." ' She bent
her head and began to sob. 'He was one in a million
was Charlie. He'd have got me the moon out of the sky
if I'd wanted it.' The girl Marilyn got up and put her
arms around her friend. 'Oh, Charlie, Charlie . . .!'

The drawer was open, Hatton's cheque book exposed. Wexford leafed through it and saw that Hatton
had paid twenty-five pounds for the lamp on May
22nd. Thirty pounds had been paid to Lucrece Ltd.,
High Street, Kingsmarkham (his wife's wedding outfit?), and another thirty in the same week, the last week
of May, to Excelsior Electrics, Stowerton (Pertwee's
record player?).

Then came three blank stubs, lastly one filled in for
fifty pounds cash. There was no stub for Vigo, the dentist. Hatton must have paid for his teeth in cash.

He put the books back in the drawer and stood waiting for Mrs. Hatton to recover. Her mother and
brother had departed to the kitchen from where
Wexford could hear their muted whisperings and the
funereally careful clink of cups.

The widow's eye make-up had transferred itself to

Marilyn Thompson's handkerchief. 'I keep breaking down,' she said. 'I can't seem to stop myself.'

'Yeah, but just reckon what you've been through, love.'

'I don't know what I'd do without you two.'

Pertwee said nothing but his baleful pugnacious look was absurd in its intensity and Wexford was almost embarrassed. He said lightly, 'Does the name McCloy mean anything to you, Mr. Pertwee?'

That it meant nothing, less than nothing, to Mrs. Hatton he was sure at once. Of Pertwee and the girl he was less certain. The latter's lower lip stuck out and her eyes flickered. For an instant she was a primitive creature looking for a hole to hide in. Pertwee had reddened, possibly only with anger at Wexford's persistence.

'Sounds Irish,' was all he said.

'Doesn't it also sound familiar?'

'Not to me, I don't know any McCloy. Never heard of him.'

'Strange then that you should have discussed this Mr. McCloy with your friends in the Dragon on Friday. Is he a local man?'

'I told you I'd never heard of him.' Pertwee bit his lip and looked down at his knees. Wexford watched him feel for the girl's hand, but she was occupied with Mrs. Hatton, dabbing at her face and smoothing her hair. Forsaken, deserted, the hand came up to Pertwee's brow and pushed into the greasy black waves. 'Can't you leave us alone now?' he pleaded and Wexford felt impotently that once again the man was enclosing himself within the unimpregnable defence of grief. 'I never knew what went on on the lorries,' he said. 'I wasn't Charlie's only friend. He had hundreds of friends. Ask Jim Bardsley, ask Cullam.' Pertwee's eyes were glazed and dull. 'Let someone else do dirt on his memory.'

Jim Bardsley had an apron tied round his waist. He moved gingerly about the kitchen, putting away crockery, as if he were afraid his touch might damage or contaminate the pristine glory of its equipment. The Hatton flat and the Cullam house had one thing in common, an automatic washing machine. Mrs. Hatton had plenty besides mixers, electric tinopeners, a steam iron as well as the huge scarlet refrigerator and the cooker with eye-level grill.

'You transport this kind of stuff, don't you, Mr. Bardsley?' Burden asked. 'I suppose Mr. Hatton got it wholesale.'

'I daresay,' Bardsley said cagily.

'Irons, electric fires and so on, was that the load you lost when Mr. Hattons' lorries were hi-jacked?' Bardsley nodded unhappily. 'Doubtless you were insured?'

'Not the second time, not in March when they knocked it off at Stamford. I had to stand the loss myself.' Bardsley untied his apron and hung up the tea cloth that, appropriately enough in this flat, was a large linen facsimile of a pound note. 'Set me back, I can tell you. I reckon poor old Charlie was glad I hadn't taken him into partnership. Mind you, they found the lorry both times. It wasn't damaged, just the stuff gone, that's all. That second time Charlie'd pulled into a lay-by and gone to sleep at the wheel. The villains didn't harm him, thank God. Just tied him up and put a gag in his mouth.'

'But he was injured on the previous occasion?'

'Had a bit of concussion,' Bardsley said. 'There wasn't any mark to show, bar a bit of a bruise.'

'Ever heard of the name McCloy, Mr. Bardsley?'

'It doesn't ring a bell,' said Bardsley and Burden believed him. 'Mind you,' he added, 'I've seen my own stuff flogged off in the market here. Known it was mine but couldn't prove it. You know what them stallholders are, up to all the tricks.' He scratched his head. 'I was a bit too nosy that time and I haven't seen the stall here since.'

'If you do, Mr. Bardsley, come straight to us. Don't argue about it, come straight to us.'

'O.K.,' said Bardsley, but without hope. Burden left

him contemplating the printed tea cloth as if, were it possible to transmute it to paper, reduce its size and multiply it manifold, he would be a happy man.

'First of all,' said Wexford, 'I'd like to know exactly how much there is in the account.'

The bank manager became pedantic and precise. 'Exactly six hundred and nine pounds, four and seven-pence.'

'I take it that's a current account? He didn't have anything on deposit, did he?'

'Unfortunately, no. When Mr. Hatton began paying large sums in I did attempt to persuade him to open one, the rate of interest being so desirable, you understand. Five per cent, as you doubtless know. But Mr. Hatton wouldn't. "I'm one for the ready, Mr. Five Per Cent," he said to me in his amusing way.' The manager sighed. 'A very likable, amusing man, poor Mr. Hatton. One of the best.'

That's a matter of opinion, Wexford thought. 'What were these large sums?'

'Really, it seems most unorthodox, but if you insist.' A large ledger was opened and horn-rimmed glasses set on the manager's nose. 'Mr. Hatton opened this account in November of last year,' he began, 'with the sum of one hundred pounds.' Payment for the first lorry hi-jacking, Wexford thought, a nice little bit of compensation for his concussion. 'Nothing was added to it until January when two separate payments of fifty pounds were made.' Two more hi-jackings, set up by Hatton, who had kept the drivers occupied at pontoon in a carmen's café? Wexford felt rather pleased. All the pieces in his puzzle were falling neatly into place. 'Then in March, March 15th, a further hundred was paid in, but no more after that until May 22nd.'

The manager paused and Wexford made a mental note to find out whether any lorries had been hi-jacked on Hatton's A.1 route during the penultimate week of May. Evidently Hatton got a hundred when he was personally involved, fifty when it was someone else to be knocked on the head and left in a ditch. Such a likable, amusing man!

'How much?' he said coldly.

The manager readjusted his glasses.

'Er ... let me see ... Good heavens. No, it isn't an error. Really, I wasn't aware ... As a matter of fact, Mr. Hatton paid five hundred pounds into his current account on May 22nd.'

And what in God's name, Wexford thought flabbergasted, did Hatton have in his power to do that was worth five hundred pounds? What could a lorry be carrying that its load was so valuable to a thief as to make Hatton's a feasible reward? There would have to be several men involved in the racket, McCloy himself, two or three men to commandeer the lorry and incapacitate the driver as well as Hatton. McCloy would want the lion's share of whatever the load realised and if Hatton, a mere decoy, got five hundred, the three henchmen would be worth at least five hundred apiece. Four times five and what for McCloy? A thousand, two thousand? That meant a cargo to the value of four or five thousand pounds. At least. For McCloy wouldn't get anything like the cargo's true value in his underworld market.

Well, it should be easy enough to find out. A hijacking of that magnitude wouldn't be likely to be quickly forgotten by the police in whose district it had occurred. He couldn't understand why he didn't recall it himself. It must have made front-page news. The last week but one in May, he repeated to himself. Presumably they'd never done anyone for the job. They certainly hadn't done Hatton.

'And after that?' he said calmly.

'Regular payments of fifty pounds a week over the past six weeks.'

Wexford checked an explosion of astonishment. 'But no more large sums?'

'No more large sums,' said the bank manager.

It was obvious what had happened. Hatton had done

his jobs for McCloy and the last one had been something spectacular. So spectacular—perhaps involving great injury or death. Why the hell couldn't he *remember* it? That Hatton, finding some weak spot in McCloy's armour, had commenced to blackmail him. A lump sum down on May 22nd and then fifty pounds a week.

It must have been nice while it lasted, Wexford reflected amorally. What was more exhilarating to a poor man than a sudden influx of unearned cash, springing from a seemingly limitless fertile source? How could such a one as Hatton restrain himself from making a splash? It came into Wexford's mind that money metaphors often have to do with water, gushing, springing, and that business men talk of liquidity and cash flow.

He came to the Kingsbrook bridge and paused for a moment on the parapet, listening to the soft suck and chatter of the stream. Everlastingly the Kingsbrook rattled over its stones, hindered here and there by tree roots or a growth of weed, but ultimately unimpeded, always moving, glittering in the sun as if gold pieces gleamed beneath its ripples.

By the water's edge Hatton had met his death. Because a source less abundant and less generous than this river had dried up?

8

'THERE ARE ONLY three McCloys in this district,' Burden said on the following morning. 'I've seen them all and they struck me as perfectly ordinary honest citizens. A couple in Pomfret are brothers. One's a teacher at the comprehensive school and the other's a lab assistant. James McCloy, who lives here in town, runs a very small unsuccessful sort of decorating business.'

'Small fry?' said Wexford, still thinking of his fish and water metaphors.

'Very small. No sign of any more money than is needed to keep the wolf from the door. Still, I've been through the trade directory and come up with something a bit more hopeful. There's a firm in London, in Deptford, calling themselves McCloy & Son Ltd., and what d'you think their line of business is?'

'*Etonne-moi,*' said Wexford after the manner of Diaghilev to Cocteau. Burden looked at him suspiciously, so he said with amused impatience, 'I don't know, Mike, and I'm not in the mood for this suspense stuff.'

'They spray the laminated surfaces on to small electrical equipment.'

'Do they, indeed?'

'I've put through a call to London and I'm waiting for them to ring me up. If there's anything at all promising I'm off to Deptford.'

'While you're waiting,' said Wexford, 'you might get on to Stamford police, Stamford in Lincolnshire. I'd like to know just what did happen when Hatton's lorry was hi-jacked on the 15th of March and if they've got any McCloys in their district.'

'Stamford, sir? Isn't there a bridge there where poor old Harold won a victory before coming a cropper at Hastings?'

'Wrong one,' said Wexford. 'This is a charming little ancient town of grey stone which the A.1 now fortunately by-passes. Shakespeare mentions it. "How a good yoke of bullocks at Stamford fair?" You might also ask them if they had a big hi-jacking at the end of May. It might not have been near them, of course, but it was so big they'll likely have heard of it."

The pretty toy of a lift had borne his weight serenely on four occasions by this time and he no longer felt much trepidation on entering it. As it sank obediently to the ground floor, he thought again about McCloy's mysterious feat of modern highwaymanship. He had checked the file of that period and found nothing. Now he too was waiting for a phone call, promised for the afternoon. Scotland Yard would enlighten him when they had consulted their records. But how could it have escaped his knowledge and the newspapers?

Sergeants Camb and Martin were gossiping in the foyer when he emerged from the lift. He gave a low cough.

'Just discussing this Fanshawe inquest, sir,' said Camb respectfully.

'I thought it had been adjourned.'

'The coroner wants to resume now, but I've told him we've nothing to go on. I'm all for waiting till Mrs. Fanshawe perks up a bit.'

'In a bad way, is she?' said Martin. Like an old woman in a supermarket queue. Wexford thought derisively.

'That accident's turned her brain, I reckon. She's no more fit to appear in court than she was six weeks ago. God knows, I can sympathise. Her husband's dead and her only child. It's not funny, I can tell you, trying to tell a sick woman her daughter's dead when she keeps insisting she's alive and in Germany.'

'Maybe she is alive,' said Wexford, more from a mischievous desire to throw a spanner in the works than from conviction. He was sick and tired of the name Fanshawe. He didn't burden the uniformed branch with his problems and he didn't see why he should have to listen to Camb's maunderings. 'Maybe it was someone else in the car.'

'Oh, no, sir; the aunt identified the girl.'

'Well, it's your problem, Sergeant. You're the coroner's officer.' Wexford added annoyingly, 'We all have our troubles and we must deal with them as best we can.' He swung open the door and said over his shoulder, 'I don't know what you think you're doing, Martin, distracting the coroner's officer in the execution of his duty. If you want a job just run upstairs and say McCloy to Mr. Burden. I'm away to the dentist myself.'

'Not in much pain, sir, I hope?'

'You're behind the times,' said Wexford, chuckling. 'You don't go to the dentist these days because you've got toothache, you go for a check-up.'

It was too fine a day for the car. Wexford crossed the road to Grover's newspaper shop and turned into York Street. In the display window of Joy Jewels the sun set the rhinestone ropes and little gilt collarets ablaze, and the plane tree leaves shadowed the pavement in damask tablecloth patterns. After the petrol station and the little houses, in one of which George Carter lived, were left behind, the street petered out into a country lane. Such was the incline of the hills at this point and the arrangement of the trees that, looking straight ahead, nothing that was not absolutely pastoral could be seen. A stranger to the district, coming over the brow of the hill, would have stopped astonished and perhaps a little peeved to see Ploughman's Lane lying beneath him.

Not that there was anything to dismay the aesthetic purist. Through the centuries about twenty-five houses had been built in Ploughman's Lane, first of all for the minor gentry, the widows and kinsmen, for instance, of the lord of the manor; in more recent times equally large and widely spaced dwellings had been put up for the professional class.

From where he stood Wexford could see roofs, a yellow patch of new thatch on the far left, red tiles some fifty yards from it, then the pinnacled and turreted grey slate so dear to the heart of the Victorian bourgeoisie; next, half lost among the spread arms of a black cedar, the pinned-down tarred fabric that roofed a split-level ranch bungalow.

He descended briskly, glad of the shade the thickening trees afforded. A Bentley swam out from behind the ranch house's tamarisk hedge, accelerated arrogantly and, passing him, drove him back flat against the hedge.

'And if I should chance to run over a cad,'

Wexford quoted,

> 'I can pay for the damage if ever so bad.
> So pleasant it is to have money, heigh ho . . . .'

God Almighty, he was getting as bad as Maurice Cullam! He had noted the number of the Bentley. Very nice cars they all had around here. There was another Bentley outside the grey slate Gothic place with a smart yellow Cortina snuggling up against it. Married bliss, thought Wexford, grinning to himself. Even the wives' cars were sizable. No minis and no second- or- third-hand jalopies. But women would never be equal, he reflected, pleased to have discovered a new profundity, until the day came when men stopped thinking it natural that their wives should always have the smaller car. And they always did, no matter how rich they were; no matter, come to that, if the wives were richer or bigger than the husbands. He tried to think of a wife who had a larger car than her husband's and he couldn't think of one. Not that he particularly wanted women to be equal. As far as that went, he was quite satisfied with the *status quo*. But to have lighted upon a new yet universal truth amused him and he went on thinking about it until he came to Jolyon Vigo's house.

The tall dark girl got off the London train and as she passed through the barrier at Stowerton station she asked the woman collecting tickets where she could get a taxi.

'There's only one. But he won't be busy at this time of day. You might be lucky. There you are! I can just see him, waiting on the rank.'

She watched the girl march briskly down the steps. Very few women as smart and cocksure as that one arrived at Stowerton station, even from London, even in the height of summer. The ticket collector, who had just had a new perm, thought the girl's geometrically cut and excessively short hair awful. It made her look like a boy, or how boys used to look in the days when

men had some self-respect and went to the barber's.
Flat-chested and skinny too, like a stick all the way
down. You had to admit, though, that that kind made
a good clothes prop. The suit she was wearing was the
colour and texture of sacking, a foreign-looking suit
somehow with those buttoned pockets, but the ticket
collector was willing to bet it hadn't cost a penny less
than forty guineas. It hardly seemed fair that a kid
of—what would she be? Twenty-three? Twenty-
four?—had forty quid to throw away on a bit of sacking. Money talks all right, she thought. It was money
that gave that snooty lift of the chin, too, that masterful
stance and walk and that stuck-up voice.

The girl approached the taxi and said to the driver:
'Will you take me to Stowerton Royal Infirmary,
please?'

When they got to the hospital she opened her brown
leather bag to pay him and he noticed that, as well as
the English money, she had some funny-looking foreign
notes in her wallet. He half hoped she would give him
one of them by mistake so that he could make a scene,
but she didn't. He summed her up as a sharp little
piece with a head on her shoulders. She was a stranger
to the place but she knew where she was going. As he
reversed, he saw her march confidently into the porter's
office.

'Can you direct me to the private wing?'

'Straight down the drive, madam, and you'll see a
notice with an arrow.' The porter called her madam because she had asked the way to the private wing. If she
had asked for Ward Five he would have told her morning visiting in the public wards was forbidden and he
might, because he was feeling benevolent, have called
her love. On the other hand, he couldn't imagine anyone like this ever wanting a public ward. She was
madam, all right, a proper little madam.

Nurse Rose was late with her bed-making on Tuesday morning. She had seen to Mrs. Goodwin by nine
o'clock and stopped for a chat and a bit of buttering-
up. You were half-way to being a lady's maid with

these private patients and if they wanted you to paint their fingernails while they told you their life histories you couldn't choose but obey. Just the same, she would have been well ahead but for those policemen turning up again and wanting to ask poor Mrs. Fanshawe more questions. Of course she couldn't make Mrs. Fanshawe's bed while they were poking about and it was nearly twelve before she managed to get the poor deluded creature into a chair and the sheets whipped off.

'It might take a letter a week to get to Germany, mightn't it?' said Mrs. Fanshawe, taking her rings off and amusing herself by making them flash in the sunlight right into Nurse Rose's eyes.

'Weeks and weeks,' said Nurse Rose, blinking. 'You don't want to worry about that.'

'I should have sent a telegram. I think I'll get you to send one for me.'

Once bitten, twice shy, thought Nurse Rose. She wasn't even going to humour Mrs. Fanshawe any more. Stick her neck out and her life would be a succession of errands for Mrs. Fanshawe, running about the town sending crazy messages to a girl who didn't exist.

'Would you like me to brush your hair?' she asked, pummelling the pillows.

'Thank you very much, my dear. You're a good girl.'

'Back into bed then. Ooh! You're as light as a feather. Don't leave those lovely rings on the table, now.'

Nurse Rose had really been very helpful, Mrs. Fanshawe thought. She didn't seem or look very intelligent, but she must be. She was the only one who didn't keep up this nonsense about Nora being dead. And how she envied her those rings! Funny little thing .... When Nora came she would get her to run up to the flat and root out that paste thing she'd once bought on a whim at Selfridges. It wasn't worth more than thirty shillings, but Nurse Rose wouldn't know that and she decided she would definitely give it to Nurse Rose.

She lay back comfortably while her hair was brushed.

'While you're getting my lunch,' she said, 'I'll think how I'm going to word my telegram. Oh, and you might take my sister's card away. It's getting on my nerves.'

Nurse Rose was glad to escape. She came out of the room, pulling her bag of soiled linen, and because she wasn't looking where she was going, almost cannoned into a tall dark girl.

'Can you tell me where I can find Mrs. Dorothy Fanshawe?'

'She's in there,' said Nurse Rose. She had never seen anything like the shoes the girl was wearing. They were of brown calf with a copper beech leaf on the instep and their shape was so strange and outlandish that Nurse Rose decided they must be the extreme of fashion. Nothing like them had ever been seen in Stowerton, nor, for that matter, Nurse Rose believed, in London. 'Mrs. Fanshawe's just going to have her lunch,' she said.

'I don't suppose it matters if that's held up for ten minutes.'

Not to you, Nurse Rose thought indignantly, whoever you may be. But she couldn't let those desirable shoes vanish without any comment and she said impulsively, 'I hope you don't mind my asking, but I do think your shoes are super. Where did you get them?'

'Nobody minds a compliment,' said the girl coldly. 'They were made in Florence but I bought them in Bonn.'

'Bonn? Bonn's in Germany, isn't it? Ooh, you can't be! You can't be Nora. You're dead!'

Earlier that morning Wexford had quoted Justice Shallow and now, as he contemplated Jolyon Vigo's house, he thought that this was just the sort of place Shallow might have lived in. It would have been a mature house already in Shakespeare's time, a 'black and white' house, timbered, solid, so perfect a place to live in that it seemed in advance to confer upon its owner a grace and taste and superiority. A climbing rose with yellow satiny flowers spread across the black striped gables and nestled against the tudor roses, carved long ago by some craftsman on every square inch of oak. On either side of the front path a knot garden had been planted with low hedges and tufts of tiny blossom. It was so neat, so unnatural in a way, that Wexford had the notion the flowers had been embroidered on the earth.

A coach-house of slightly later vintage served as a double garage. It had a small belvedere and a vertical sundial under its pediment. The garage doors were open—a single untidy touch—and within Wexford saw two cars. Again it amused him to note the general application of what he was beginning to think of as Wexford's Law. A woman was in the act of opening the door of a pale blue Minor. She slammed it and, carrying a child in her arms, squeezed between the small vehicle and the huge, finned Plymouth, dragonfly blue, that stood a foot from it.

The phrase 'a woman with a child' somehow suggested a peasant and a shawled baby. Eyeing her, Wexford thought that to say a lady with an infant would be better.

'What d'you want?' she said in the sharp high-pitched voice of the local gentry. Before she could add, as she was evidently about to, that she never bought anything at the door, he announced himself hurriedly and asked for her husband.

'He's in the surgery. You go round by the pleached walk.'

Marvelling that anyone could say this without a trace of selfconsciousness or humour, Wexford looked her up and down. She was a plain young woman, thin and dark with a worn face. She put the child into a pram and wheeled it down the path. The boy was big and handsome, blue-eyed and fair-headed. He looked as though by being born he had sapped his mother's strength and left her a used-up husk. Wexford was reminded of a butterfly, fresh and lusty, that has escaped from a dried chrysalis.

He was not precisely sure what a pleached walk was, but when he came upon it there was no mistaking it and, smiling to himself, he descended a flagged step and passed into a green tunnel. The trees whose branches met and interwove above his head were apples and pears and already the young green fruit hung abundantly. The walk led to some greenhouses and what had once been a stable, now converted into a surgery. Amid all this sylvan glory the notice giving the dentist's working hours struck a discordant note. Wexford opened a latched horse-box door and entered the waiting room.

A pretty girl in a white coat came out to him and he reminded her of his appointment. Then, having no inclination for *Elle* or *Nova*, he sat down and viewed the room.

It was a funny place for Charlie Hatton to have found himself in and Wexford wondered why he hadn't attended the dentist in the town. On these walls were none of the usual posters bidding young mothers to drink milk in pregnancy and bring their toddlers for a twice-yearly check-up. Nor was there any notice explaining how to get dental treatment on the National Health Service. You couldn't imagine anyone sitting here with a handkerchief pressed to a swollen jaw.

The walls were papered in a Regency stripe and the one or two pieces of upholstered furniture looked like genuine antiques. The curtains were of dark chintz patterned with medallions. A small chandelier caught the sun and made rainbow spot patterns on the ceiling. Wexford thought the place was just like the sitting room of a person of taste. There were dozens like it in Kingsmarkham. But this was just a dentist's waiting room and it made him wonder what the rest of the house would be like. He was in for a surprise. He was admiring a stylish flower arrangement, observing how cunningly a spray of jasmine had been made to tremble half in, half out of the vase and trail against the console table, when the girl came back and told him Mr. Vigo would see him now.

Wexford followed her into the surgery.

There was nothing out of the ordinary here, just the usual chairs and trays of instruments and contraptions of tubes and clamps and wires. Ice-blue blinds were lowered to keep out the noonday sun.

Vigo was standing beside one of the windows, fingering some instruments in a tray, and when Wexford came in he didn't look up. Wexford smiled dryly to himself. This air of being always overworked, preoccupied by esoteric matters was, he knew, characteristic of some doctors and dentists. It was part of the mystique. In a moment Vigo would glance round, show surprise and make some swift apology for being engaged on matters beyond a policeman's comprehension.

The dentist had a fine leonine head, the hair fair and abundant. His jaw was strong and prominent, the mouth thin. One day when he was old this would be a nutcracker face but that was a long way off. He seemed to be counting and when he had finished he turned and reacted as Wexford had expected he would.

'Do forgive me, Chief Inspector. A little matter that couldn't be left. I understand you want to talk to me about the late Mr. Hatton. I've no more patients until after lunch, so shall we go into the house?'

He took off his white coat. Under it he was wearing a slate-blue suit in tussore, the cut, material and colour not quite masculine enough for his height and heavily muscled chest. He had the figure of a rugby international and he made Wexford, who was just on six feet, feel short.

Wexford followed him through the pleached walk and they entered the house by a glazed garden door. It was like stepping into a museum. Wexford hesitated, dazzled. He had heard of Chinese rooms, heard of Chinese Chippendale, but he had never seen a room furnished in the style. The brilliance of its colours turned the remembered garden outside into monochrome. His feet sank into a carpet whose blues and creams evoked a summer sky and, at Vigo's behest, he lowered himself uneasily into a chair with a yellow satin seat and legs of rearing dragons. The dentist moved with apparent carelessness between tables and cabinets loaded with china and jade and stood, a faint smile on his thin lips, under a long picture of red fish painted on silk.

'I don't know what you can have to ask me about Mr. Hatton's teeth,' he said. 'He didn't have his own teeth.'

Wexford had come to talk business and yet for a moment he could not. Talk of false teeth in this setting? His eye fell on a set of chessman ranged on a table in a far corner. They were two armies, one of ivory, one of red jade, and the pawns were on horseback, the white armed with spears, the red with arrows. One of the red knights on a panoplied charger had a contemporary Western face, a raw sharp face which called to mind absurdly that of Charlie Hatton. It grinned at Wexford, seeming to prompt him.

'We know that, Mr. Vigo,' he said, wrenching his eyes away and fixing them on an eggshell thin service, made to contain jasmine tea. 'What surprises us is that a man of his means should have such superb false ones.'

Vigo had an attractive, rather boyish laugh. He checked it with a shake of his head. 'A tragedy, wasn't it? Have you any idea who could have . . . ? No, I mustn't ask that.'

'I've no objection to your asking, but no, we've no idea yet. I've come to you because I want you to tell me everything you can about Mr. Hatton with particular reference to anything you may know about the source of his income.'

'I only know that he drove a lorry.' Vigo was still savouring with pride and joy his caller's astonishment. 'But yes, I see what you mean. It surprised me too. I don't know much but I'll tell you what I can.' He moved to a cabinet whose door handles were the long curved tails of dragons. 'Will you join me in a pre-luncheon sherry?'

'I don't think so, thank you.'

'Pity.' Vigo didn't press him but poured a glass of Manzanilla for himself and sat down by the window. It gave on to a shadowed court whose centrepiece was an orrery on a stone plinth. 'Mr. Hatton made an appointment with me at the end of May. He had never been a patient of mine before.'

The end of May. On the 22nd of May Hatton had paid five hundred pounds into his bank account, his share, no doubt, of the mysterious and elusive hi-jacking haul.

'I can tell you the precise date, if you like. I looked it up before you came. Tuesday, 21st May. He telephoned me at lunchtime on that day and by a fluke I had a cancellation, so I was able to see him almost immediately. He'd had dentures since he was twenty, very bad ill-fitting ones, by the way. They made him self-conscious and he wanted a new set. I asked him why he'd lost his own teeth and he said the cause had been pyorrhoea. Knowing a little of his circumstances by this time—at any rate, I knew what his job was—I asked him if he realised this would involve him in considerable expense. He said that money was no object—those were his actual words—and he wanted the most expensive teeth I could provide. We finally arrived at a figure of two hundred and fifty pounds and he was perfectly agreeable.'

'You must have been surprised.'

Vigo sipped his sherry reflectively. He touched one of the chessmen, a crenellated castle, caressing it with pride. 'I was astonished. And I don't mind telling you I was a little uneasy.' He didn't elaborate on this unease but Wexford thought he must have been worried lest the two hundred and fifty wasn't forthcoming. 'However, the teeth were made and fitted at the beginning of June. About a month ago it would have been."

'How did Mr. Hatton pay you?'

'Oh, in cash, he paid me on the same day, insisted on

doing so. The money was in five-pound notes which I'm afraid I paid straight into my bank. Chief Inspector, I understand what you're getting at, but I couldn't ask the man where he got his money from, could I? Just because he came here in his working clothes and I knew he drove a lorry . . . I couldn't.'

'Did you ever see him again?'

'He came back once for a check. Oh, and a second time to tell me how pleased he was.'

Again Wexford was becoming bemused by the colours, by the seductive spectrum that caught and held his eye wherever he looked. He bent his head and concentrated on his own big ugly hands. 'On any of his visits,' he said stolidly, 'did he ever mention someone called McCloy?'

'I don't think so. He spoke about his wife and his brother-in-law that he was in business with.' Vigo paused and searched his memory. 'Oh, and he mentioned a friend of his that was getting married. I was supposed to be interested because the chap had sometimes been here doing electrical repairs. Hatton said something about buying him a record player for a wedding present. The poor fellow's dead and I don't know whether I ought to say this . . .'

'Say on, Mr. Vigo.'

'Well, he did rather harp on what a lot of money he spent. I don't want to sound a snob but I thought it vulgar. He only mentioned his wife to tell me he'd just bought her something new to wear and he tried to give me the impression his brother-in-law was something of a poor fish because he couldn't make ends meet.'

'But the brother-in-law was in the same line of business.'

'I know. That struck me. Mr. Hatton did say he had a good many irons in the fire and that sometimes he brought off a big deal. But frankly, if I thought about that at all, I imagined he had some side line, painting people's houses perhaps or cleaning windows.'

'Window cleaners don't speak of bringing off big deals, Mr. Vigo.'

'I suppose not. The fact is I don't have many dealings with people of Mr. Hatton's . . .' Vigo paused. Wexford was sure he had been about to say 'class'. 'Er, background,' said the dentist. 'Of course you're suggesting the side lines weren't legitimate and this may be hindsight, but now I look back Mr. Hatton did perhaps occasionally have a shady air about him when he talked of them. But really it was only the merest nuance.'

'Well, I won't trouble you any further.' Wexford got up. It must be his over-sensitive suspicious mind that made him see a relieved relaxing of those muscled shoulders. Vigo opened the carved oak door for him.

'Let me see you out, Chief Inspector.' The hall was a largish square room, its flagged floor dotted with thin soft rugs, and every inch of burnished ancient wood caught the sunlight. There were Blake prints on the walls, the Inferno scenes, Nebuchadnezzar with his eagle's talons, the naked Newton with his golden curls. Stripped of his blue tussore, Vigo himself might look rather like that, Wexford thought. 'I had the pleasure of a visit from your daughter the other day,' he heard the dentist say. 'What a lovely girl she is.'

'I'm told she's much admired,' Wexford said dryly. The compliment slightly displeased him. He interpreted it as spurious and ingratiating. Also there had been a note of incredulity in Vigo's voice as if he marvelled at such an old goose begetting a swan.

The front door swung open and Mrs. Vigo came in, holding the child. For the first time since his arrival, Wexford remembered that there was another child, a mongol, confined somewhere in an institution.

The baby which Vigo now took in his arms was perhaps six or seven months old. No one could have doubted its paternity. Already it had its father's jaw and its father's athletic limbs. Vigo lifted the boy high, laughing as he chuckled, and there came into his face an intense besotted adoration.

'Meet my son, Mr. Wexford. Isn't he splendid?'

'He's very like you.'

'So they tell me. Looks more than seven months, doesn't he?'

'Going to be a big chap,' said the chief inspector. 'Now that we've each complimented the other on his handsome offspring, I'll take my leave, Mr. Vigo.'

'A mutual admiration society, eh?' Vigo laughed heartily but his wife's face remained grave. She took the boy from him roughly as if so much exaggerated worship offended her. Again Wexford thought of the mongol whose fate no amount of money could change. Grief fills the room up of my absent child, lies in his bed, walks up and down with me ...

Wexford went out into the sunshine and the knot garden.

9

THE CALL FROM Scotland Yard came through half an hour after Wexford got back to the station. In the whole country only two lorries had been hi-jacked during the latter part of May and neither was on Hatton's regular route. One had been in Cornwall, the other in Monmouthshire, and they had been loaded with margarine and tinned peaches respectively.

Wexford looked at the memo Burden had left him before departing for Deptford:

'Stamford say no records of any thefts from lorries in their area during April or May.'

It was unlikely that Hatton could have had a hand in the Cornwall or Monmouthshire jobs. Margarine and tinned fruit! Even if there had been tons of it, a fourth or fifth share couldn't have amounted to five hundred pounds. Besides, wasn't he underestimating Hatton's haul? He had banked five hundred on May 22nd, *drawn out* twenty-five pounds for the lamp. Another sixty had gone on clothes and the record player. And all this while, Wexford guessed, Hatton had been living like a king. True, the first and perhaps the second blackmail payments had come in before he was obliged to pay for his teeth at the beginning of June, but he had blithely paid two hundred and fifty for them in cash when the demand came.

Surely that meant that although Hatton had banked only five hundred on May 22nd, he had in fact received more, perhaps even twice that sum. He carried notes about with him in his wallet, on one occasion, at any rate about a hundred pounds.

Suppose there had been no mammoth hi-jacking at the end of May? That would mean that all Hatton's wealth had been acquired through blackmail, and blackmail entered into not as the consequence of a hi-jacking but of something else.

There was a lot more to this, Wexford thought with frustration, than met the eye.

'There seems to be a lot more to this than meets the eye,' said Sergeant Camb indignantly. 'Mrs. Fanshawe's own sister identified the dead young lady as Miss Nora Fanshawe.'

'Nevertheless,' the girl said, 'I am Nora Fanshawe.' She sat down on one of the red spoon-shaped chairs in the station foyer and placed her feet neatly together on the black and white tiles, staring down at the shoes Nurse Rose had so gushingly admired. 'My aunt was probably very strung up and you say the girl was badly burned. Very disfigured, I suppose?'

'Very,' said Camb unhappily. His immediate superior and his superintendent had departed ten minutes before for a conference at Lewes and he was more than somewhat at a loss. What the coroner was going to say to all this he dreaded to think.

'Mrs. Fanshawe's sister seemed quite certain.' But had she? He remembered the scene quite vividly, taking the woman into the mortuary and uncovering the faces, Jerome Fanshawe's first and then the girl's. Fanshawe had been lying on his face and the fire had scarcely touched him. Besides, the woman had recognised the silver pencil in his breast pocket, his wristwatch and the tiny knife scar, relic of some schoolboy ritual, on that wrist. Identifying the girl had been so extremely distasteful. All her hair had been burnt away but for the black roots and her features hideously charred. It made him shudder to think of it now, hardened as he was.

'Yes, that's my niece,' Mrs. Browne had said, recoiling and covering her own face. Of course he had asked her if she was quite certain and she had said she was, quite certain, but now he wondered if it was mere association that had made her agree, association and horror. She had said it was her niece because the girl was young and had black hair and because who else but Nora Fanshawe could have been in that car with her parents? Yet someone else had been ... And what the hell was the coroner going to say?

His eyes still seeing the charred appalling face, he turned to the young hard untouched face in front of him and said:

'Can you prove you're Nora Fanshawe, miss?'

She opened the large hide handbag she was carrying and produced a passport, handing it to Camb without a word. The photograph wasn't much like the girl who sat on the other side of the desk, but passport photographs seldom are much like their originals. Glancing up at her uneasily and then back to the document in front of him he read that Nora Elizabeth Fanshawe, by profession a teacher, had been born in London in 1945, had black hair, brown eyes and was five feet nine inches tall with no distinguishing marks. The girl in the mortuary hadn't been anything like five feet nine, but you couldn't expect an aunt to tell the height of a prone corpse.

'Why didn't you come back before?' he asked.

'Why should I? I didn't know my father was dead and my mother in hospital.'

'Didn't you write? Didn't you expect them to write to you?'

'We were on very bad terms,' the girl said calmly. 'Besides, my mother did write. I got her letter yesterday and I took the first plane. Look here, my mother knows me and that ought to be enough for you.'

'Your mother . . .' Camb corrected himself. 'Mrs. Fanshawe's a very sick woman . . . .'

'She's not mad if that's what you mean. The best thing will be for me to phone my aunt and then perhaps you'll let me go and have something to eat. You may not know it, but I haven't had a thing to eat since eight o'clock and it's half-past two now.'

'Oh, I'll phone Mrs. Browne,' Camb said hastily. 'It wouldn't do for her to hear your voice just like that. O dear, no.' He was half convinced.

'Why me?' said Wexford. 'Why do I have to see her? It's nothing to do with me.'

'You see, sir, the super and Inspector Letts have gone to Lewes . . .'

'Did the aunt recognise her voice?'

'Seemed to. She was in a bit of a way, I can tell you. Frankly, I don't have much faith in the aunt.'

'Oh, bring her up,' Wexford said impatiently. 'Anything to make a change from lorries. And, Camb—use the lift.'

He had never seen her mother or her aunt so he couldn't look for family resemblances. But she was a rich man's daughter. He looked at the bag, the shoes, the platinum watch and, more than anything, he sensed about her an air, almost repellent, of arrogance. She wore no scent. He took from her in silence the passport, the international driver's licence and Mrs. Fanshawe's letter. It occurred to him as he turned them over that Nora Fanshawe—if she was Nora Fanshawe—probably stood to inherit a vast sum of money. Jerome Fanshawe had been an affluent stockbroker. It might be that this girl was a con woman and he and Camb the first victims of a colossal deception.

'I think we had better have an explanation,' he said slowly.

'Very well. I don't quite know what you want.'

'Just a moment.' Wexford took Camb aside. 'Was there nothing but this Mrs. Browne's word to identify the dead girl?' he asked rather grimly.

Camb looked downcast. 'There was a suitcase in the car with clothes in it,' he said. 'We went through the contents of two handbags we found in the road. One was Mrs. Fanshawe's. The other had nothing in it but some make-up, a purse containing two pounds and some silver and a packet of cigarettes.' He added defensively, 'It was a good expensive handbag from Mappin and Webb.'

'My God,' said Wexford in disgust, 'I just hope you haven't landed us with a female Tichborne claimant.' He went back to the girl, sat down on the opposite side of the desk and gave a brisk nod. 'You went on holiday with Mr. and Mrs. Fanshawe to Eastover?' he asked. 'On what date was that?'

'May the 17th,' the girl said promptly. 'I am a teacher of English at a school in Cologne and I gave up my job at the end of March and returned to England.'

'Since when you have been living with Mr. and Mrs. Fanshawe?'

If the girl noticed that he didn't refer to them as her parents she gave no sign. She sat stiff and tense with her finely sculpted head held high. 'Not at first,' she said and he sensed a faint diffidence creep into her voice. 'My parents and I hadn't been on good terms for some time. I went back to live with them—or rather, to stay with them—in the middle of May. My mother wanted me to go down to the bungalow with them and because I wanted—I wanted our relations to improve—well, I said I would.' Wexford nodded noncommittally and she went on. 'We all drove down to Eastover on Friday, May 17th . . .' Her shoulders stiffened and she looked down at her folded hands. 'That night I had a disagreement with my parents. Is there any need for me to go into details?' Without waiting for Wexford's consent to her reticence, she swept the quarrel aside and said, 'I felt it was useless to try and patch things up. We were worlds apart, we . . . The result was that on the Saturday morning, I told my mother there was nothing for me in England and I was going back to Germany to try and get my old job back. I took one of the suitcases of clothes I had brought with me and went to Newhaven to get the boat for Dieppe.'

'And did you get your old job back?'

'Fortunately I did. There's a shortage of teachers in Germany as well as here and they were only too glad to see me. I even got my old room back in the *Goethestrasse*.'

'I see. Now I should like the name and address of the authority who employ you, the name of your landlady and that of the school in which you've been teaching.'

While the girl wrote this information down for him, Wexford said:

'Weren't you surprised to hear nothing from Mr. or Mrs. Fanshawe during the past six weeks.

She looked up and raised her straight, rather heavy, black eyebrows. 'I told you we'd quarrelled. My father would have expected an abject apology from me, I assure you, before he condescended to write.' It was the first show of emotion she had made and it did more to make Wexford believe her story than all the documentary evidence she had furnished him with. 'These silences were commonplace with us,' she said. 'Especially after a set-to like the one we had that night. Six months could have gone by. Why should I imagine any harm had come to them? I'm not clairvoyant.'

'But you came as soon as Mrs. Fanshawe wrote.'

'She is my mother, after all. Now do you suppose I might go and get myself some lunch?'

'In a moment,' Wexford said. 'Where are you planning to stay?'

'I was going to ask you to recommend somewhere,' the girl said a shade sardonically.

'The Olive and Dove is the best hotel. I suggest you get in touch immediately with your late father's solicitors.'

The girl got up and not a crease marked the skirt of her suit. Her self-confidence was almost stupefying. Camb opened the door for her and with a crisp 'Good afternoon' she took her leave of them. As her footsteps died away, the sergeant burst out miserably:

'If she's Nora Fanshawe, sir, who, for God's sake, was the girl in the road?'

'That's your problem, Sergeant,' Wexford said unkindly.

'It could well be yours, sir.'

'That's what I'm afraid of. Haven't I got enough with a murder on my hands?'

Lilian Hatton was an easier nut to crack than the girl who called herself Nora Fanshawe. She broke down and wept bitterly when Wexford told her that her husband's supplementary income had come from a criminal source. He was almost sure that it was all a revelation to her and he watched her in sad silence as she covered her face and shook with sobs.

'I have been given your husband's log book by your brother, Mrs. Hatton,' he said gently as she recovered herself. 'Now I also want to know if you keep any sort of diary or engagement book yourself.'

'Just a pad by the phone,' she gulped, 'where I kind of jot things down.'

'I'm going to ask you if you'll kindly let me borrow that.'

'You think,' she began, dabbing at her eyes as she came back with the pad, 'you think someone—someone killed my Charlie because he wouldn't go on—go on doing these jobs for them?'

'Something like that.' Now was not the time to suggest to this woman that her husband had been a blackmailer as well as a thief. 'Who knew Mr. Hatton would pass along the Kingsbrook path that night?'

She twisted the damp hankerchief in hands whose nails were still pitifully and bravely painted the way Charlie Hatton had liked them, red and shiny and glittering. 'All the darts club,' she said. 'And me—I knew. My mum knew and my brother, Jim. Charlie always came that way back from the pub.'

'Mrs. Hatton, did your husband ever receive any callers in this flat that you didn't know? Strangers, I mean, that he wanted to talk to alone?'

'No, he never did.'

'Perhaps when you were out? Can you ever remember your husband asking you to go out and leave him alone with anyone?'

The handkerchief was torn now, sopping wet and useless as an absorbent. But she put it to her eyes and brought it away streaked black and green. 'When he was home,' she said, 'I never went out. We always went out together. We was like—like inseparable. Mr. Wexford . . .' She gripped the arms of her chair and two red flame-like spots burned in her cheeks. 'Mr. Wexford, I've heard all you've said and I've got to believe it. But whatever my Charlie did, he did it for me. He was a husband in a million, a good kind man, a wonderful man to his friends. You ask anyone, ask Jack . . . . He was one in a million!'

Oh! withered is the garland of war! The soldier's poll is fallen . . . . Strange, Wexford thought, that when you considered Charlie Hatton you thought of war and soldiers and battles. Was it because life itself is a battle and Hatton had waged it with unscrupulous weapons, winning rich spoils and falling as he marched home with a song on his lips?

How sentimental he was getting! The man was a blackmailer and a thief. If life was a battle and Charlie Hatton a soldier of fortune he, Wexford, stood in the position of a United Nations patrol whose job it was to prevent incursions on the territory of the defenceless.

'I don't want to ask you anything more now, Mrs.

Hatton,' he said to the widow as he left her weeping among the dead man's ill-gotten glories.

In the High Street he encountered Dr. Crocker emerging from Grover's with a copy of the *British Medical Journal*.

'Been making any good arrests lately?' asked the doctor cheerfully. 'Now, now, mind your hypertension. Want me to take your blood pressure? I've got my sphyg in the car.'

'You know what you can do with your sphyg,' said Wexford, proceeding to tell him in lurid detail. 'I reckon just about the whole population of Kingsmarkham knew Charlie Hatton would be taking the field path home that night.'

'No reason why it should be a local man, is there?'

'I may not be a wizard with a sphygmomanometer,' said Wexford derisively, 'but I'm not daft. Whoever killed Charlie Hatton knew the lie of the land all right.'

'How come? He'd only got to be told by Charlie that he'd be leaving the High Street by the bridge and walking along the local river.'

'You think? You reckon Hatton would also have told him the river bed was full of stones one of which would make a suitable weapon for knocking off his informant?'

'I see what you mean. There could be one or more brains behind the killing but whoever struck the blow, albeit a henchman, was Kingsmarkham born and bred.'

'That's right, Watson. You're catching on. My old mate,' Wexford remarked to no one in particular, 'albeit a sawbones, is coming on.' Suddenly his voice dropped and tapping the doctor's arm, his face hardening, he said, 'D'you see what I see? Over there by the Electricity Board?'

Crocker followed his gaze. From Tabard Road a woman wheeling a pram had emerged in Kingsmarkham High Street and stopped outside a plate-glass display window of the Southern Electricity Board. Presently two more children joined her, then a man holding a third child by the hand and another in his arms. They remained in a huddle on the pavement, staring at the dazzling array of kitchen equipment as if hypnotised.

'Mr. and Mrs. Cullam and their quiverful,' said Wexford.

The family were too far away for their conversation, an apparently heated and even acrimonious discussion, to be audible. But it was evident that an argument was taking place between the adults, possibly as to whether their need of a refrigerator was greater than their desire for a mammoth room heater. The children were taking sides vociferously. Cullam shook one of his daughters, cuffed his elder son on the head, and then they all plunged into the showroom.

'Will you do something for me?' Wexford asked the doctor. 'Go in there and buy a light bulb or something. I want to know what that lot are up to.'

'What, spy on them and report back, d'you mean?'

'Charming way you put it. That's what I spend my life doing. I'll sit in your car. Can I have the keys?'

'It's not locked,' Crocker said awkwardly.

'Is that so? Well, don't come screaming to me next time one of the local hippies pinches a load of your acid off you. Go on. A forty watt bulb and we'll reimburse you out of petty cash.'

The doctor went unwillingly. Wexford chuckled to himself in the car. Crocker's cautious approach to the electricity showroom, his quick sidelong glances, called to mind days long gone by when Wexford, then a sixth-form boy, had witnessed this same man as a child of ten, scuttling up to front doors playing 'Knocking Down Ginger'. In those days the infant Crocker had run up paths lightly and gleefully to bang on a knocker or ring a bell and, elated with an enormous naughtiness, hidden behind a hedge to see the angry householder erupt and curse. There was no hedge here and Crocker was fifty. But as he entered the showroom, had he too experienced a flash of memory, a stab of nostalgia?

Jesu, Jesu, thought Wexford, once more evoking Jus-

tice Shallow, the mad days that I have spent! And to
see how many of my old acquaintance are dead . . . .
Enough of that. On the lighter side it reminded him of
Stamford and he wondered how Burden had got on.
Somehow a little business in Deptford didn't quite
match up with his own ideas of McCloy's origins.

Samantha Cullam scuttled out on to the pavement.
Her mother came next, lugging the pram. When the
whole brood were assembled their father regimented
them with a series of fortunately ill-aimed blows and
they all trailed off the way they had come. Then
Crocker appeared, duplicity incarnate.

'Well?'

'Don't snap at me like that, you saucy devil,' said the
doctor, immensely pleased with himself. 'I set traps, as
the Psalmist says, I catch men.'

'What did Cullam buy?'

'He didn't exactly *buy* anything, but he's after a refrigerator.'

'Getting it on the H.P. is he?'

'Money wasn't mentioned. They had a bit of a ding-
dong, Mr. and Mrs., and one of the kids knocked a Py-
rex dish off a cooker. That brute Cullam fetched him a
fourpenny one, poor little devil. They're all keen on
getting this fridge, I can tell you.'

'Well, what about these traps you laid?'

'That was just a figure of speech,' said the doctor.
'Didn't I do all right? I bought the bulb like you said.
One and nine if you don't mind. I'm not in this for my
health.'

10

'THEY CALL THEMSELVES McCloy Ltd.,' Burden said wearily, 'but the last member of the firm of that name died twenty years ago. It's an old established set-up, but I reckon it's on its last legs now. In this so-called affluent society of ours folks buy new stuff, they don't want this reconditioned rubbish.'

'You can say that again,' said Wexford, thinking of Cullam.

'The Yard put me on to six other McCloys all more or less in the hardware business or on its fringes. Not a smell of anything fishy about one of them. Stamford have given me a list of local McCloys and there again not a sniff as far as they know. But I'll be off to Stamford in the morning to have a scent round. The local force have promised me all the help I need.'

Wexford lounged back in his swivel chair and the dying sun played on his face. 'Mike,' he said, 'I wonder if we haven't been starting from the wrong end. We've been looking for McCloy to lead us to his hired assassin. We might do better to find the hired assassin and let him lead us to McCloy.'

'Cullam?'

'Maybe. I want Martin to be Cullam's shadow and if he goes and pays cash for that refrigerator we're really getting somewhere. Meanwhile I'm going to make Hatton's log book and Mrs. Hatton's engagement book my homework for tonight. But first, how about a quick one at the Olive and Dove?'

'Not for me thanks, sir. I haven't had an evening in

for a week now. Divorce is against my wife's principles but she might get ideas as to a legal separation.'

Wexford laughed and they went down in the lift together. The evening was warm and clear, the light and the long soft shadows more flattering to this market town High Street than the noonday sun. The old houses were at their best in it, their shabbiness, the cracks in their fabric veiled, as an ageing face is veiled and smoothed by candlelight. By day the alleys than ran into a scruffy hinterland were rat-hole rubbish traps but now they seemed romantic lanes where lovers might meet under the bracket lamps and as the sun departed, watch the moon ride over a Grimm's fairy tale huddle of pinnacled rooftops.

As yet it was only eight o'clock and the sun reluctant to leave without treating its worshippers to a pyrotechnic display of rose and gold flames that burnt up the whole western sky. Wexford stood on the south side of the bridge and listened to the river chuckling. Such an innocent river, for all that it knew a secret, for all that one of its stones had put a man out of sight of the sunset!

All the street windows of the Olive and Dove were open, the curtains fanning out gently over window boxes and over fuchsias that dripped red flowers. On the forecourt a band of Morris dancers had assembled. They wore the motley coat of jesters and one of them was hopping around on a hobby horse. To his amusement Wexford picked out George Carter among the company.

'Lovely night, Mr. Carter,' he said jovially. Rather shame-facedly Carter waved at him a stick with ribbons and bells on. Wexford went into the saloon bar.

At a table in the alcove on the dining-room wall sat the girl Camb had brought to him earlier in the day, an elderly woman and a man. Wexford brought his beer and as he passed them the man got up as if to take his leave.

'Good evening,' Wexford said. 'Have you decided to stay at the Olive?'

The girl was sparing with her smiles. She nodded sharply to him and said, naming his rank precisely, 'I'd like to you meet my father's solicitor, Mr. Updike. Uncle John, this is Detective Chief Inspector Wexford.'

'How do you do?'

'And I don't think you've met my aunt, Mrs. Browne?'

Wexford looked from one to the other. Marvellous the way he always had to do Camb's work for him! The aunt was looking pale but excited, the solicitor gratified. 'I'm quite prepared to accept that you're Miss Fanshawe now, Miss Fanshawe,' Wexford said.

'I've known Nora since she was so high,' said Updike. 'You need have no doubt that this is Nora.' And he gave Wexford a card naming a London firm, Updike, Updike and Sanger of Ava Maria Lane. The chief inspector looked at it, then again at Mrs. Browne who was Nora Fanshawe grown old. 'I'm satisfied.' He passed on to an empty table.

The solicitor went to catch his train and presently Wexford heard the aunt say:

'I've had a long day, Nora. I think I'll just give the hospital a ring and then I'll go up to bed.'

Wexford sat by the window, watching the Morris dancers. The music was amateurish and the performers self-conscious, but the evening was so beautiful that if you shut your eyes to the cars and the new shop blocks you might imagine yourself briefly in Shakespeare's England. Someone carrried out to the nine men a tray of bottled beer and the spell broke.

'Come into the lounge,' said a voice behind him.

Nora Fanshawe had removed the jacket of her suit and in the thin coffee-coloured blouse she looked more feminine. But she was still a creature of strong straight lines and planes and angles and she was still not smiling.

'May I get you a drink, Miss Fanshawe?' Wexford said, rising.

'Better not.' Her voice was abrupt and she didn't thank him for the offer. 'I've had too much already.'

And she added with a dead laugh, 'We've been what my aunt calls celebrating. The resurrection of the dead, you see.'

They went into the lounge, sat down in deep cretonne-covered armchairs and Nora Fanshawe said:

'Mr. Updike wouldn't tell me the details of the accident. He wanted to spare me.' She beckoned to the waiter and said without asking Wexford first, 'Bring two coffees.' Then she lit a king-sized cigarette and slipped it into an amber holder. 'You tell me about it,' she said.

'You don't want to be spared?'

'Of course not. I'm not a child and I didn't like my father.'

Wexford gave a slight cough. 'At about ten o'clock on May 20th,' he began, 'a man driving a petrol tanker on the north to south highway of Stowerton by-pass saw a car overturned and in flames on the fast lane of the south to north track. He reported it at once and when the police and ambulance got there they found the bodies of a man and a girl lying on the road and partially burned. A woman—your mother—had been flung clear on to the soft shoulder. She had multiple injuries and a fractured skull.'

'Go on.'

'What remained of the car was examined but, as far as could be told, there was nothing wrong with the brakes or the steering and the tyres were nearly new.'

Nora Fanshawe nodded.

'The inquest was adjourned until your mother regained consciousness. The road was wet and your mother has suggested that your father may have been driving exceptionally fast.'

'He always drove too fast.' She took the coffee that the waiter had brought and handed a cup to Wexford. He sensed that she would take it black and sugarless and he was right. 'Since the dead girl wasn't I,' she said with repellently faultless grammar, 'who was she?'

'I'm hoping you'll be able to tell us that.'

She shrugged, 'How should I know?'

Wexford glanced at the curled lip, the hard direct eyes. 'Miss Fanshawe,' he said sharply, 'I've answered your questions, but you haven't even met me half-way. This afternoon you came to my office as if you were doing me a favour. Don't you think it's time you unbent a little?'

She flushed at that and muttered. 'I don't unbend much.'

'No, I can see that. You're twenty-three, aren't you? Don't you think all this upstage reserve is rather ridiculous?'

Her hand was small, but, ringless and with short nails as it was, it was like a man's. He watched it move towards the cup and saucer and for a moment he thought she was going to take her coffee, get up and leave him. She frowned a little and her mouth hardened.

'I'll tell you about my father,' she said at last. 'It might just help. I first knew about his infidelities when I was twelve,' she began. 'Or, let me say, I knew he was behaving as other people's fathers didn't behave. He brought a girl home and told my mother she was going to stay with us. They had a row in my presence and when it was over my father gave my mother five hundred pounds.' She took the cigarette stub from her holder and replaced it with a fresh one. This sudden chain smoking was the only sign she gave of emotion. 'He bribed her, you understand. It was quite direct and open. "Let her stay and you can have this money." That was how it was. The girl stayed six months. Two years later he bought my mother a new car and at just the same time I caught him in his office with his secretary.' She inhaled deeply. 'On the floor,' she said coldly. 'After that it was an understood thing that when my father wanted a new mistress he paid my mother accordingly. By that I mean what he thought the girl was worth to him. He wanted my mother to stay because she was a good hostess and kept house well. When I was eighteen I went up to Oxford.

'After I got my degree I told my mother I could

keep her now and she should leave my father. Her response was to deny everything and to tell my father to stop my allowance. He refused to stop it—mainly because my mother had asked him to, I suppose. I haven't drawn it for two years now, but ...' She glanced swiftly at her bag, her watch. 'You can't always refuse to take presents,' she said tightly, 'not when its your own mother, not when you're an only child.'

'So you took a job in Germany?' Wexford asked.

'I thought it would be as well to get away.' The flush returned, an unbecoming mottled red. 'In January,' she said hesitantly, 'I met a man, a salesman who made business trips to Cologne from this country.' Wexford waited for her to talk of love and instead heard her say with a strange sense of shock, 'I gave up my job, as I told you, and came back to London to live with him. When I told him that if we were to be married I wouldn't ask my father for a penny he ... well, he threw me out.'

'You returned to your parents?'

Nora Fanshawe raised her head and for the first time he saw her smile, an ugly harsh smile of self-mockery. 'You're a cold fish, aren't you?' she said surprisingly.

'I was under the impression you despised sympathy, Miss Fanshawe.'

'Perhaps I do. Want some more coffee? No, nor do I. Yes, I went back to my parents. I was still sorry for my mother, you see. I thought my father was older now and I was older. I knew I could never live with them again, but I thought ... Family quarrels are uncivilised, don't you think? My mother was rather pathetic. She said she'd always wanted a grown-up daughter to be real friends with.' Nora Fanshawe wrinkled her nose in distaste. 'Even upstage reserved characters like myself have their weak spots, Chief Inspector. I went to Eastover with them.'

'And the quarrel, Miss Fanshawe?'

'I'm coming to that. We'd been on surprisingly good terms up till then. My father called my mother darling once or twice and there was a kind of Darby and Joan air about them. They wanted to know what I was doing about getting another job and all was serene. So serene, in fact, that after we'd had a meal at the bungalow and a few drinks my mother did something she'd never done before. My father had gone off up to bed and she suddenly began to tell me what her life with him had been, the bribery and the humiliation and so on. She really talked as if I were a woman friend of her own age, her confidante. Well, we had about an hour of this and then she asked me if I had any romantic plans of my own. Those were her words. Like a fool I told her about the man I'd been living with. I say like a fool. Perhaps if I hadn't been a fool I would have been the dead girl on the road.'

'Your mother reacted unsympathetically?'

'She goggled at me,' said Nora Fanshawe, emphasising the verb pedantically. 'Then, before I could stop her she got my father out of bed and told him the whole thing. They both raved at me. My mother was hysterical and my father called me a lot of unpleasant names. I stood it for a bit and then I'm afraid I said to him that what was sauce for the gander was sauce for the goose and at least I wasn't married.' She sighed, moving her angular shoulders. 'What do you think he said?'

'It's different for men,' said Wexford.

'How did you guess? At any rate, for once my parents presented a united front. After my mother had obligingly betrayed all my confidences to him in my hearing, he said he would find the man—Michael, that is—and compel him to marry me. I couldn't stand any more, so I locked myself in my bedroom and in the morning I went to Newhaven and got on the boat. I parted from my mother just about on speaking terms. My father had gone out.'

'Thank you for unbending, Miss Fanshawe. Have you been suggesting that the dead girl might have been your father's mistress?'

'You think it impossible that my father would drive

his wife and mistress together to London? I assure you it's not unlikely. For him it would simply have been a matter of bringing the girl along, telling my mother she was coming with them and paying her handsomely for the hardship occasioned.'

Wexford kept his eyes from Nora Fanshawe's face. She was as unlike his Sheila as could be. They had in common only their youth and health and the fact, like all women, of each being someone's daughter. The girl's father was dead. In a flash of unusual sentimentality, Wexford thought he would rather be dead than be the man about whom a daughter could say such things.

In a level voice he said, 'You gave me to understand that as far as you know there was no woman at the time but your mother. You have no idea who this girl could be?'

'That was the impression I had. I was evidently wrong.'

'Miss Fanshawe, this girl clearly could not have been a friend or neighbour at Eastover whom your parents were simply driving to London. In that case her relatives would have enquired for her, raised a hue and cry at the time of the accident.'

'Surely that would apply whoever she was?'

'Not necessarily. She could be a girl with no fixed address or someone whose landlady or friends expected her to move away about that particular weekend. She may be listed somewhere among missing persons and no search have begun for her because the manner of her life showed that occasional apparent disappearances were not unusual. In other words, she could be a girl who led a somewhat itinerant life in the habit of taking jobs in various parts of the country or moving about to live with different men. Suppose, for instance, she had spent the weekend in some South Coast resort and tried to hitch a lift back to London from your father?'

'My father wouldn't have given a lift to anyone. Both he and my mother disapproved of hitch-hiking. Chief Inspector, you're talking as if everyone in that car is now dead. Aren't you forgetting that my mother is very much alive? She's well on the way to recovery and her brain isn't affected. She insists there was no one in the car but my father and herself.' Nora Fanshawe lifted her eyes and her voice lost some of its confidence. 'I suppose it's possible she could be having some sort of psychological block. She wants to believe my father was a changed man, that no girl was with them, so she's convinced herself they were alone. That could be it.'

'I'm sure it must be.' Wexford got up. 'Good night, Miss Fanshawe. Thank you for the coffee. I take it you'll be staying here a few days?'

'I'll keep in touch. Good night, Chief Inspector.'

The next step, he thought as he walked home, would be to investigate the missing persons list in the holiday towns and London too, if those proved fruitless. That was routine stuff and not for him. Why, anyway, was he following this road accident that wasn't even properly his province to distract his mind from the urgency of the Hatton affair? Because it had features so distracting and so inexplicable that no-one could simply explain them away?

Of course it would turn out that the dead girl was merely someone Jerome Fanshawe had come across that weekend and who had taken his fancy. Nothing so dramatic as Nora Fanshawe had suggested need have happened. Why shouldn't Fanshawe just have said to his wife, 'This young lady has missed her last train and since she lives in London I said we'd give her a lift? But in that case Mrs. Fanshawe would hardly deny the girl's presence.

There was more to it than that. There was the handbag. Camb had searched that handbag and found in it nothing but make-up and a little money. That wasn't natural, Wexford reflected. Where were her keys? Come to that, where were all the other things women usually stuff into bags, handkerchiefs, dress shop bills, receipts, tickets, pen, letters? The things which were there were anonymous, the things which were not there were the objects by which someone might be identified.

Wexford let himself into his own house and the dog Clytemnestra galloped to meet him.

'What would you do,' Wexford said to his wife, 'if I brought a young girl home and offered you a thousand pounds to let her stay?'

'You haven't got a thousand pounds,' said Mrs. Wexford.

'True. There's always a fly in the ointment.'

'On the subject of young girls and money, Mr. Vigo has sent a whacking bill for your daughter's tooth.'

Wexford looked at it and groaned. 'Pleached walks!' he said. 'Chinese Chippendale! I just hope one of my customers pinches her orrery, that's all. Is there any beer in the house?'

Suppressing a smile, his wife stepped over the now recumbent form of the knitted dog and went into the kitchen to open a can.

A pewter tankard at his elbow, Wexford spent the next couple of hours studying Hatton's log book and Mrs. Hatton's engagement diary.

It was the week immediately preceding May 21st which interested him. On the 22nd Hatton had paid five hundred pounds into his bank and two days prior to that had either been in possession of a large sum of money or confident of acquiring it, for on the 21st, a Tuesday, he had ordered his new set of teeth.

Mrs. Hatton's engagement diary was a calendar in the shape of a rectangular book. The left-hand pages bore a coloured photograph of some English beauty spot with an appropriate verse, both for the picture and the time of year, while the right-hand pages were each divided into seven sections. The days of the week were listed on the left side and a space of perhaps on inch by five was allowed for brief jottings.

Wexford opened it at Sunday, May 12th.

The photograph was of Kentish fruit orchards and the lines beneath it from *As You Like It*: 'Men are

April when they woo, December when they wed. Maids are May while they are maids, but the sky changes when they are wives.' Not true of the Hattons, he thought. Now to see how Mrs. Hatton had occupied herself during that particular week.

Nothing for Sunday. Monday May 13th: *C. left for Leeds. Mother to tea.* Tuesday May 14th: *Rang Gas Board. C. home 3 p.m. Pictures.* And here in Hatton's log book was the Leeds trip confirmed. He had stopped twice on the way up, at Norman Cross for lunch at the Merrie England café, and at Dave's Diner near Retford for a cup of tea. His room in Leeds was with a Mrs. Hubble at 21 Ladysmith Road, and on the return journey he had stopped only once and again at the Merrie England. There was nothing in the log book at this stage to make Wexford even pause. Hatton had done the journey in the shortest possible time, leaving no possible spare moment for undercover activities. He turned back to the diary.

Wednesday, May 15th: *C. off work. Rang doctor. Mem, N.H.S., not private.* Interesting. Hatton had been ill and at that time apparently not in funds. Thursday May 16th: *C. summer flu. Ring Jack and Marilyn put off dinner.* There was no entry for Friday, May 17th.

Saturday, May 18th: *C. better. Doctor called again. Jim and mother came.*

That completed the week. Wexford turned the page to Sunday, May 18th: *C left for Leeds. Mem, will ring me 8 p.m. J and M came for drinks and solo game.* Opposite was a photograph of a large country house and the lines: 'It is a truth universally acknowledged that a single man in possession of a good fortune must be in want of a wife.' Wexford smiled grimly to himself. Monday, May 20th: *C. bad again. Left Leeds late. Home 10 p.m.*

Quickly Wexford checked with the log book. Yes, here was Hatton's entry that he had been too ill to start the return journey until noon. He had driven home slowly and stopped twice on the way at the Hollybush at Newark and at the Merrie England. But had he really been ill or had he been shamming, crafty sick to give himself extra time in Leeds? For however he acquired that money he must have acquired it, Wexford was certain, during the 19th or the 20th of May.

Tuesday, May 21st: *C. fit again. Day off. Saw Jack and Marilyn. Appointment 2 p.m. with dentist.*

A precise little woman, Lilian Hatton, if not exactly verbose. Impossible to tell if she knew anything. The last place to which she would have confided her secrets was this calendar diary.

It didn't look as if Hatton had been up to much on that Monday morning in Leeds, but you never knew. There was always the night between Sunday and Monday to be considered. For all Wexford knew or could remember there might have been a bank robbery in that city at that time. It would all have to be checked. He wondered why the Fanshawe business kept intruding and upsetting his concentration, and then suddenly he knew.

Fanshawe had crashed his car on Monday, May 20th; an unidentified girl had died on May 20th and also on May 20th something big had happened to Charlie Hatton.

But there couldn't be a connection. Fanshawe was a wealthy stockbroker with a flat in Mayfair and, apart from a bit of moral nastiness, not a stain on his character. Charlie Hatton was a cocky little lorry driver who had probably never set foot in Mayfair all his life.

It was just a curious coincidence that Hatton had been killed on the day following that of Mrs. Fanshawe's regaining consciousness.

Wexford closed the books and emptied his tankard for the third time. He was tired and fanciful and he had drunk too much beer. Yawning ponderously, he put Clytemnestra outside the back door and while he waited for her, stood staring emptily at the cloudless, star-filled sky.

11

'GOOD MORNING, MISS Thompson,' Wexford said with a heartiness he didn't feel.

'Mrs. Pertwee, if you don't mind.' She picked up one of the wire baskets that were stacked outside the supermarket and gave him a selfconscious, defiant stare. 'Jack and me got married very quietly yesterday afternoon.'

'May I be among the first to offer my congratulations?'

'Thanks very much, I'm sure. We didn't tell no one about it, just went off to church quietly by ourselves. Jack's been so cut up about poor Charlie. When are you going to catch his killer, that's what I want to know? Not putting yourselves out, I reckon, on account of him being a working fella. Been different if he was one of your upper crust. This capitalist society we live in makes me spit, just spit it does.'

Wexford backed a little, fearing she might suit the action to the word. The bride snapped her bootbrush eyelashes at him. 'You want to pull your socks up,' she said relentlessly. 'Whoever killed Charlie, hanging'd be too good for him.'

'Dear, oh dear,' said Wexford mildly, 'and I thought you progressives were dead against capital punishment.'

She banged into the supermarket and Wexford went on his way, smiling wryly. Camb eyed him warily as he entered the police station.

'Getting interested in this Fanshawe business, I gather, sir. I met Miss Fanshawe on my way in.'

'So interested,' Wexford said, 'that I'm sending Detective Constable Loring down to find out who's missing in the holiday towns and it might be worth our while to check with London too.'

Burden had left for Stamford. Stepping into the lift, Wexford decided to do the London checking himself. Young women were beginning to get on his nerves. There were so many of them about, and it seemed to him they caused as much trouble to a policeman as burglars. Now to see how many of them were missing in London. This task was for him somewhat *infra dig*, but until Burden and Sergeant Martin brought him some information he had little else to do, and this way he could, at any rate, be certain it was well done.

By lunchtime he had narrowed his search down to three out of the dozens of girls missing in the London area. The first was a Carol Pearson, of Muswell Hill, interesting to him because she had worked as a hairdresser's improver at a shop in Eastcheap. Jerome Fanshawe's office was in Eastcheap and the hairdresser's had a barber's shop attached to it. Hers was also a significant name because she had black hair and her disappearance was reported on May 17th.

The second girl, Doreen Dacres, was like Carol Pearson, black-haired and aged twenty, and his interest was aroused because she had left her room in Finchley on May 15th to take a job in Eastbourne. Nothing further had been heard of her either in Finchley or at the Eastbourne club address.

Bridget Culross was the last name with which he felt he need concern himself. She was twenty-two years old and had been a nurse at the Princess Louise Clinic in New Cavendish Street. On Saturday May 18th she had gone to spend the weekend with an unnamed boy friend in Brighton, but had not returned to the clinic. It was assumed that she had eloped with her boy friend. Her hair was also dark, her life erratic and her only relative an aunt in County Leix.

Young women! Wexford thought irritably, and he thought also of his own daughter who was making him scrape the bottom of his pocket so that at some future possible never-never time she might be able to smile without restraint before the cameras.

The long day passed slowly and it grew very hot. Clouds massed heavily, dense and fungoid in shape, over the huddled roofs of the town. But they did nothing to diminish the heat, seeming instead to enclose it and its still, threatening air under a thick muffling lid. The sun had gone, blanked out by sultry vapour.

To an observer Wexford might be thought only to be sitting, like many other inhabitants of Kingsmarkham, waiting for the storm to break. He did nothing. He lay back by the open window with his eyes closed and the warm breathless air came to him just as in another cooler season heat fanned from the grid lower down the wall. No one disturbed him and he was glad. He was thinking.

In Stamford, where it was raining, Inspector Burden went to a country house supposedly occupied by a man named McCloy and found it deserted, its doors locked and its garden overgrown. There were no neighbours and no one to tell him where McCloy had gone.

Detective Constable Loring drove along the promenades of the south coast towns, calling at police stations and paying particular attention to those clubs and cafés and amusement halls where girls come and go and pass each other. He had found a club where Doreen Dacres had been engaged but where no Doreen Dacres had arrived and this comforted him. He even telephoned Wexford to tell him about it, his elation subsiding somewhat when he heard the chief inspector had also found this out three hours before.

The storm broke at five o'clock.

For some time before this heavy clouds had increased and in the west the sky had become a dense purplish-black, a range of mountainous cumulus against which the outlines of buildings took on a curious clarity and the trees stood out livid and sickly bright. In spite of the clammy heat, shoppers began to hurry, but the rain which fell so readily when rainy days preceded it, after a fortnight's drought, held off as if it could only be squeezed out as a result of some acute and agonising pressure. It was as though the clouds were not themselves mere vapour but impermeable sagging sacks, purposely constructed and hung to contain water.

The first whispering breeze came like a hot breath and Wexford closed his windows. Almost imperceptibly at first the trees in the High Street pavement began to sway. Most of the merchandise outside greengrocers' and florists' had already been taken in and now it was the turn of the sunblinds to be furled and waterproof awnings to take their place. The air seemed to press against Wexford's windows. He stood against them, watching the dark western sky and the ash-blue cumulus now edged with brilliant white.

The lightning was the forked kind and it branched suddenly like a firework and yet like the limb of a blazing tree. As its fiery twigs flashed out and cut into the inky cloud, the thunder rolled out of the west.

Wexford dearly loved a storm. He liked the forked lightning better than the zig-zag kind and now he was gratified by a second many-branched display that seemed to spring and grow from the river itself, blossoming in the sky above the Kingsbrook meadows. This time the thunder burst with a pistol-shot snap and with an equal suddenness, as if at last those swollen vessels had been punctured, the rain began to fall.

The first heavy drops splashed in coin shapes on the pavement below and in their tubs the pink flowers on the forecourt dipped and swayed. For a brief moment it seemed that the rain still hesitated, that it would only patter dispiritedly on the dust-filled gutters where its drops rolled like quicksilver. But then, urged on as it were by a series of multiple lightning flashes, it hesitated no more and, instead of increasing gradually from the first tentative shower, the water gushed forth in a vast fountain. It dashed against the windows, washing off dust in a great cleansing stream, and Wexford moved away from the glass. The sudden flood was more like a wave than rain and it blinded the window as surely as darkness.

He heard the car splash in and the doors slam. Burden, perhaps. The internal phone rang and Wexford lifted the receiver.

'I've got Cullam here, sir.' It was Martin's voice. 'Shall I bring him up? I thought you might like to talk to him.'

Maurice Cullam was afraid of the storm. That didn't displease Wexford. With some scorn he eyed the man's pale face and the bony, none-too-steady hands.

'Scared, Cullam? Not to worry, we'll all die together.'

'Big laugh,' said Cullam, and he winced as the thunder broke above their heads. 'I don't reckon it's safe being so high up. When I was a kid I was in a house that got struck.'

'But you got out unscathed, eh? Well they say the devil looks after his own. Why have you brought him here, Sergeant?'

'He's bought that refrigerator,' said Sergeant Martin. 'And a room heater *and* a load of other electrical bits and pieces. Paid cash for them, a couple of quid short of a hundred and twenty pounds.'

Wexford put the lights on and behind the streaming glass the sky looked black as on a winter's night. 'All right, Cullam, where did you get it?

'I saved it up.'

'I see. When did you buy that washing machine of yours, the one you washed your gear in after Hatton died?'

'April.' As the storm receded and the thunder became a distant grumbling. Cullam's shoulders dropped and he lifted sullen eyes. 'April, it was.'

'So, you've saved another hundred and twenty pounds in just two months. What do you get a week? Twenty? Twenty-two? You with five kids and council house rent to pay? You've saved it in two months?

Come off it, Cullam. I couldn't save it in six and my kids are grown up.'

'You can't prove I didn't save it.' Cullam gave a slight shiver as the overhead light flickered off, then on again. A rolling like the banging of many drums, distant at first, then breaking into a staccato crackling, announced the return of the storm to Kingsmarkham. He shifted in his chair, biting his lip.

Wexford smiled as a zig-zag flash changed the gentle illumination of the office into a sudden white blaze. 'A hundred pounds,' he said. 'That's pathetic payment for a man's life. What's your worth, Sergeant?'

'I'm insured for five thousand, sir.'

'That's not quite what I meant, but we'll let it pass. You see, an assassin is paid according to his own self-valuation. Never mind what the victim's life's worth. If a road sweeper kills the king he can't expect to get the same gratuity as a general. He wouldn't expect it. His standards are low. So if you're going to employ an assassin and you're a mean skin-flint you pick on the lowest of the low to do your dirty work. Mind you, it won't be so well done.'

Wexford's last words were drowned in thunder. 'What d'you mean, lowest of the low?' Cullam lifted abject yet truculent eyes.

'The cap fits, does it? They don't come much lower than you, Cullam. What, drink with a man—drink the whiskey he paid for—and then lie in wait to kill him?'

'I never killed Charlie Hatton!' Cullam leapt trembling to his feet. The lightning flared into his face and, covering his eyes with one hand, he said desperately, 'For God's sake can't we go downstairs?'

'I reckon Hatton was right when he called you an old woman, Cullam,' Wexford said in disgust. 'We'll go downstairs when I'm good and ready. You talk and when you've told me where McCloy is and what he paid you, then you can go downstairs and hide your head.'

Still on his feet, Cullam leant on the desk, his head

hanging. 'It's a lie,' he whispered. 'I don't know McCloy and I never touched Hatton.'

'Where did the money come from then? Oh, sit down, Cullam. What sort of man are you, anyway, scared of a bit of thunder? It's laughable, afraid of a storm but brave enough to wait in the dark down by the river and bash your friend over the head. Come on now, you may as well tell us. You'll have to sooner or later and I reckon this storm's set in for hours. Hatton had fallen foul of McCloy, hadn't he? So McCloy greased your palm a bit to walk home with Hatton and catch him unawares. The weapon and the method were left to you. Curious, you were so mean, you even grudged him a proper cosh.'

Cullam said again, 'It's all a lie.' He twisted down into the chair, holding his head and keeping it averted from the window. 'Me bash Charlie on the head with one of them stones? I wouldn't have thought of it . . . I wouldn't . . .'

'Then how did you know it was a river stone that killed him?' Wexford pounced triumphantly. Slowly Cullam raised his head and the sweat glistened on his skin. 'I didn't tell you.'

'Nor me, sir,' said the sergeant.

'Jesus,' Cullam said, his voice uneven and low.

The black clouds had parted to show between them shreds of summer sky turned sickly green. Against the glass the unremitting rain pounded.

Stamford police knew nothing of Alexander James McCloy. His name was on the voter's list as occupying Moat Hall, the small mansion Burden had found deserted, but plainly he had left it months before. Burden plodded through the rain from estate agent to estate agent and he at last found Moat Hall, listed in the books of a small firm on the outskirts of the town. It had been sold in December by McCloy to an American widow who, having changed her mind without ever living in the place, had returned it to the agent's hands and departed to spend the summer in Sweden.

Mr. McCloy had left them no address. Why should he? His business with them had been satisfactorily completed; he had taken his money from the American lady and disappeared.

No, there had never really been anything in Mr. McCloy's behaviour to make them believe he wasn't a man of integrity.

'What do you mean, "really"?' Burden asked.

'Only that the place was never kept decently as far as I could see, not the way a gentleman's house should be. It was a crying shame to see those grounds neglected. Still, he was a bachelor and he'd no staff as far as I know.'

Moat Hall lay in a fold of the hills perhaps a mile from the A.1. 'Was he always alone when you saw him at the house?' Burden asked.

'Once he had a couple of chaps with him. Not quite up to his class I thought.'

'Tell me, were you taken all over the house and grounds to make your survey or whatever you do?'

'Certainly. It was all quite above board—none too clean, but that's by the way. Mr. McCloy gave me a free hand to go where I chose, bar the two big outhouses. They were used for stores he said, so there was no point in me looking. The doors were padlocked anyway and I got what I wanted for my purpose from looking at the outside.'

'No stray lorries knocking about, I daresay?'

'None that I saw.'

'But there might have been in the outhouses?'

'There might at that,' said the agent doubtfully. 'One of them's near as big as a hangar.'

'So I noticed.' And Burden thanked him grimly. He was almost certain that he had found him, that he could say, 'Our McCloy was here,' and yet what had he achieved but dredge up a tiny segment of McCloy's life? The man had been here and had gone. All they could do now was to turn Moat Hall upside down in the forlorn hope something remained in the near-dere-lict place to hint at its erstwhile owner's present refuge.

'Are you going to charge me with murdering him?' Cullam said hollowly.

'You and McCloy and maybe a couple of others when you've told us who they are. Conspiracy to murder, the charge'll be. Not that it makes much difference.'

'But I've got five kids!'

'Paternity never kept anyone out of jail yet, Cullam. Come now, you wouldn't want to go inside alone, would you? You wouldn't want to think of McCloy laughing, going scot-free, while you're doing fifteen years? It'll be the same sentence for him, you know. He doesn't get off any lighter just because he only told you to kill Hatton.'

'He never did,' Cullam said wildly. 'How many times do I have to tell you I don't know this McCloy?'

'A good many times before I'd believe you. Why would you kill Hatton on your own? You don't have to kill a man because he's got more money and a nicer home than you have.'

'I didn't kill him!' Cullam's voice came dangerously near a sob.

Wexford switched off the light and for a moment the room seemed very dark. Then, as his eyes grew accustomed, he saw that it was no darker than on any summer evening after heavy rain. The light had a cold bluish tinge and the air was cooler too. He opened the window and a light fresh breeze clutched at the curtains. Down below on the forecourt the tub flowers had been flattened into a sodden pink mush.

'Listen, Cullam,' he said, 'you were there. You left the bridge ten minutes before Hatton started. It was twenty to eleven when you said goodbye to Hatton and Pertwee and even walking none too fast you should have been indoors at home by eleven. But you didn't get in till a quarter past. The following morning you washed the shirt you'd been wearing, the pullover and the trousers. You knew a river stone had been used to kill Hatton and today you, who get twenty pounds a week and never have a penny to bless yourself with, spent a hundred and twenty quid on luxury equipment. Explain it away, Cullam, explain it away. The storm's blowing over and you've nothing to worry about except fifteen years inside.'

Cullam opened his big ill-made hands, clenched them and leant forward. The sweat had dried on his face. He seemed to be having difficulty in controlling the muscles which worked in his forehead and at the corners of his mouth. Wexford waited patiently, for he guessed that for a moment the man was totally unable to speak. Terror had dried and paralysed his vocal chords. He waited patiently, but without a vestige of sympathy.

'The hundred quid and his pay packet,' Cullam said at last. His tone was hoarse and terrified. 'I ... I took it off his body.'

12

'WHAT DID HE want it for, Charlie-bloody-Hatton? I've been in his place, I've seen what he'd got. You ever seen his wife, have you? Got up like a tart with her new frocks and her jewellery and all that muck on her face, and not a bleeding thing to do all day long but watch that colour telly and ring up her pals. They hadn't got no kids, yelling and nagging at you the minute you get in, crawling all over you in the night because they're cutting their bloody teeth. You want to know when my missus last had a new frock? You want to know when we last had a night out? The answer's never, not since the first baby come. My missus has to buy the kids' clothes down the jumble sale and if she wants a pair of nylons they come off the Green Shield stamps. Bloody marvellous, isn't it? Lilian Hatton's got more coats than a perishing film star but she has to go and spend thirty quid on a new outfit for Pertwee's wedding. A hundred pounds? She wouldn't even miss it. She could use it for spills to light her fags.'

The flood-gates had opened and now Cullam, the reticent, the truculent, was speaking without restraint and from a full heart. Wexford was listening with concentration, but he did not appear to be listening at all. If Cullam had been in a fit state to observe behaviour he might have thought the chief inspector bored or preoccupied. But Cullam only wanted to talk. He was indifferent to listeners. All he required was the luxury of silence and a nearly empty room.

'I could have stuck it all,' he said, 'but for the bragging. "Put it away, Maurice," he'd say. "Your need's greater than mine," and then he'd tell me about the new necklace he'd bought for his missus. "Plenty more where that came from," he'd say. Christ, and I can't find the money to buy my kids new shoes! Two kids I'd got when I'd been married as long as Hatton. Is it fair? Is it right? You tell me.'

'I've listened to the party political broadcast,' said Wexford. 'I don't give a damn for your envy. Envy like yours is a hell of a good motive for murder.'

'Yeah? What would I get for killing him? I wasn't in his will. I've told you what I did. I took the money off his body. Five kids I've got and the milkman don't come till eleven in the morning. You ever tried keeping milk for five kids without a fridge in a heatwave?' He paused and with a shifty, fidgety look, said, 'D'you know what Hatton'd have done that Saturday if he hadn't been killed? Wedding first, Pertwee's wedding, and Hatton all got up in a topper with his tarty wife. Round the shops afterwards, not to buy anything, just to fritter. Charlie told me it wasn't nothing for them to get through twenty nicker poking about in the shops. Bottle of wine here, some muck for her face there. Then they'd have some more booze at the Olive, have dinner. Off to the pictures the evening and in the best seats. Bit of a contrast from me, isn't it? If I want to relax I go out in the garden, anywhere to get away from the kids' bawling.'

'Are you a Catholic, Cullam?'

That surprised him. He had perhaps been expecting a tougher comment and he hunched his shoulders, muttering suspiciously, 'I haven't got no religion.'

'Don't give me that stuff about children then. Nobody makes you have children. Ever heard of the pill? My God, they knew how to plan families twenty years, thirty years before you were born.' Wexford's voice grew hard as he warmed to a favourite theme. 'Having kids is a privilege, a joy, or it should be, and, by God, I'll get the County down on you if I see you strike that boy of yours on the head again! You're a bloody animal, Cullam, without an animal's ... Oh! what's the use? What the hell are you doing anyway, cluttering up my office, wasting my time? Cut the sob stuff and tell me what happened that night. What happened when you left Hatton and Pertwee at the bridge?'

Stamford had promised to give Burden all the help they could and they were as good as their word. A sergeant and a constable went back with him to Moat Hall and the locks on the two outhouses were forced.

Inside they found oil on the concrete floor and, imprinted by that oil, a tracery of tyre marks. Apart from that there was nothing to show a suspect occupancy but two crushed cardboard cases in one corner. Both had contained canned peaches.

'No joy here,' said Burden to the sergeant. He threw the flattened cardboard down in disgust. 'I've got things like this in my own garage at home. The supermarket gives them to me to bring my wife's shopping home in on Fridays.'

He came to the doorway and started across the deserted yard. As surely as if he could see them actually arriving, see them now, he pictured the stolen lorries driven in. The big doors would open for them and close on them and McCloy and the men who were 'not quite up to his class' would unload them and store the cargoes here. Back-slapping, laughing immoderately, Charlie Hatton would go into the house for a drink and a 'bite to eat' before driving the lorry away and abandoning it.

'I'd like to go over the house,' he said, 'only breaking and entering's not in my line. We'll have to wait for permission from the expatriate lady in Sweden.'

Cullam got up and wandered to the window. He looked as if he expected Wexford to hinder him, but Wexford said nothing.

'He was flashing all this money about in the Dragon. On and on about it he was when we walked up to the bridge.' Cullam stood by the window, staring fixedly now at the road he had trodden with Hatton and Pertwee. The wet pavements cast back mirror reflections. Wexford guessed the Kingsbrook must have swollen now, its stones submerged under a mill-race. 'Pertwee told me to wait for Charlie Hatton,' Cullam said. 'I wouldn't do that. God, I was sick of him and his money.' Slowly he pushed a hand through his thin tow-coloured hair. 'Anyway, I told you, I wasn't feeling too good. I just walked along the path in the dark.'

Thinking of what you were going home to, Wexford thought, and what Hatton was. There would have been no sound down there but the sibilant trickle of water. Above Cullam, above the web of black branches, a tranquil galaxy, a net of stars. Greed and envy took from a man's heart everything but—well, greed and envy. If Cullam had noticed anything as he walked it would have been the rubbish, the flotsam that the river sucked in and gathered on its journey through the meadows.

'Did you wait for him?'

'Wait, nothing!' Cullam said hotly. 'Why would I? I hated his guts.' Wexford wondered how long since anyone had made so many damaging admissions in this office in so short a space of time. Cullam burst out violently. 'I was sick then. I threw up under the trees. And I felt bloody, I can tell you.' He shuddered a little, but whether at the memory of this vomiting by the water's edge or of something even uglier Wexford could not tell. He watched the man narrowly, not caring for the wariness of his eyes and the way his hands had begun to twitch. 'I'm not used to whisky. A half of bitter's more my line.'

'You're not the only one,' Wexford said sharply. 'What happened then? Did you hear Hatton approach?'

'I'd heard him for a bit by then. I could hear him whistling a long way behind. He was whistling that stupid little old song of his about the man who was scared to go home in the dark.' Wexford looked up and met the shifty eyes. They slid away furtively, the pink lids blinking. Was Cullam a complete clod or did he realise how macabre his words had been? A man would have to be totally deficient in imagination to fail to be struck with a kind of horror and awe.

> 'Mabel, dear,
> Listen here,
> There's robbery in the park . . .'

Burden, who had heard them, had memorised the words and repeated them to his chief. 'Robbery in the park . . .' How did it go on? Something about there being no place like home but he couldn't go home in the dark. It was Wexford's turn to shiver now. In spite of his age, his experience, he felt a cold thrill run through him.

'Then it happened,' Cullam said suddenly. His voice trembled. 'You're not going to believe this, are you?'

Wexford only shrugged.

'It's the truth. I swear it's the truth.'

'Save your swearing for the dock, Cullam.'

'Christ . . .' The man made a sudden effort and the words tumbled out fast. 'The whistling stopped. I heard a sort of sound . . .' He had no descriptive power, few adjectives but hackneyed obscenities. 'A kind of choking, a sort of—well, God, it was horrible! I felt so bloody bad, anyway. After a bit I got up and—and I went back. I was scared stiff. It was sort of creepy down there. I couldn't see nothing and I—I stumbled over him. He was lying on the path. Could I have a drink of water?'

'Don't be a damned fool,' Wexford snapped.

'You needn't be so rough with me,' Cullam whined, 'I'm telling you, aren't I? I don't have to tell you.'

'You have to, Cullam.'

'I struck a match,' the man mumbled. 'Charlie's head was all bashed in. I turned him over and I got blood on me.' The words slurred and he gabbled. 'I don't know what come over me. I put my hand inside his coat and took hold of that wallet. There was a hundred quid in it, just on a hundred. He was all warm . . .'

Wexford stared at him aghast. 'He was dead, though?'

'I don't know . . . I don't . . . Christ, yes, he was dead! He must have been dead. What are you trying to do to me?' The man put his head in his hands and his shoulders shook. Wexford took hold of his jacket roughly, pushing him so that his head jerked up. The tears on Cullam's cheeks awoke in him a nausea and a rage so fierce it was all he could do to prevent himself from striking him. 'That's all, everything,' Cullam whispered, shuddering. 'The body rolled down the slope into the water. I ran home then, I ran like hell.' He put his fists into his eyes like a child. 'It's all true,' he said.

'The stone, Cullam, what about the stone?'

'It was laying by him. By his legs. I don't know why but I chucked it back in the water. There was blood on it and hair, bits of hair and—and other bits. . .'

'A bit late in the day to get squeamish, wasn't it?'

Wexford's tone was savage, its effect electric. Cullam sprang to his feet and let out a great cry, drumming his fists on the desk.

'I never killed him, I never, never . . . ! You've got to believe me.'

Burden had just come in, damp and disgruntled, when Wexford erupted bull-like from the lift.

'Where's Martin?'

'Don't ask me. I've just driven close to two hundred miles and I . . .'

'Never mind all that. I've got Cullam upstairs and he's come out with a fine tale.' Controlling his voice with an effort, he gave Burden a swift précis. 'Says he took the money off Hatton's corpse. Maybe that's all he did. I just don't know.'

'But you'll hold him? Keep him here on a charge of stealing the hundred quid and the pay packet?'

'Something like that. Martin can deal with it. I want you and Loring and anyone else going spare over in Sewingbury to turn Cullam's house upside down.'

'In case he's got McCloy's blood money hidden away?'

'Mike, I'm just beginning to wonder,' Wexford said wearily, 'if McCloy isn't a myth, a fiction. Cullam's a damned liar and all we know of McCloy rests on his word alone. Why shouldn't he have fabricated McCloy as a neat little red herring?' He sighed. 'Only he hasn't got any imagination,' he said.

'McCloy exists all right,' Burden said emphatically. 'He's an elusive sort of bird but he exists.'

It was eleven when Wexford got home. They had searched Cullam's house, grubbing through soiled un-made beds, cupboards full of clothes that smelt of food spills, drawers containing a jumble of broken rubbish. They had searched but the only money they had found was two and eightpence in Mrs. Cullam's handbag, a white plastic handbag with black grease in its creases. And their only sinister discovery was bruises and con-tusions on the legs of one of the children. . . .

'Give me an ounce of civet, good apothecary,' said Wexford to Clytemnestra, 'to sweeten my imagination.' In the belief that he had told her she was a good dog, Clytemnestra wagged her plumed grey tail. The door opened and Sheila came in. "What are you doing home on a Wednesday?' said her father ungraciously.

'That thing came off my tooth. I was eating a Milky Way and it collapsed. So I had to come down and see Mr. Vigo.' She gave him a disarming smile and kissed his cheek. Her hair was dressed in a pyramid of fat ringlets and she looked like a Restoration wench, maid to Millamant, scene stealer, fit to be kissed in corners.

'Well, did he fix it up?'

'Mm-hm. On the spot. He said he wouldn't charge me.'

'Charge you? Me, you mean. And I should hope not.'

Wexford grinned, sloughing off the memory of Cullam's filth like a soiled skin. 'Now you've got false teeth,' he said, 'you mustn't expect to eat toffee.'

'I haven't got false teeth. I've just got a crown. D'you want some of my coff-choc? it's Nes and drinking chocolate mixed up. Quite groovy.'

'I don't think so, lovely, thanks all the same.'

'Mr. Vigo and I got quite matey,' said Sheila. She dropped on the floor and, lying on her stomach with her elbows on the carpet, looked up into his face. He gave me tea in that Chinese room of his. I was scared to move, he's obviously so crazy about all that stuff. His wife came and banged the door and he was furious because it made the china rattle; he said she just didn't understand.'

'How quaint. What you might call a new one.'

'Oh, Pop, it wasn't like that. When I went the receptionist was just leaving and she walked down into the town with me. She said Mr. Vigo had really married for money. She was an heiress and she had a hundred thousand pounds and Mr. Vigo wanted money to collect that Chinese stuff. He only stays with his wife now because of the baby. And he goes away most weekends. Sometimes he doesn't come back till quite late on Monday night. The receptionist thinks he's got a girl friend in London. She seemed a bit jealous. D'you know, I got the idea he sleeps with her too.'

Wexford kept his face unmoved, but for the faintest flicker of what he hoped looked like sophisticated amusement. He wasn't shocked by what he had been told; he was astonished that it should have been said to him by his own daughter. In a way he was proud and grateful. Nearly forty years had passed since he was Sheila's age. Could he have spoken such words to his father? He would rather have died.

Sheila stretched, got up easily. 'Since I'm home,' she said, 'I may as well do my duty. Fancy ten minutes down by the river, dog?'

Wexford said quickly, 'No, not there, sweetheart.'

'What, allow his child to walk alone by those dark waters? I'll take the dog.'

'Really?'

'Go on. Get off to bed. That hair looks as though it'll take a lot of coping with.'

Sheila giggled. 'You'd be surprised.' He stared, somewhat appalled, as she lifted the wig like a hat and dropped it over a cut-glass vase.

'My God, it's a wise father that knows his own child!' He eyed her eyelashes suspiciously, her long fingernails. How many more bits were take-off-able? Wexford, who was hardly ever shaken from his equilibrium by the devious excesses of criminals, was perpetually astonished by his own daughter. Smiling wryly, he fetched the lead and yanked Clytemnestra from the best armchair.

The night air was fresh, washed by the storm into a cool clarity. Hardly a star showed, for the sky was veiled by a lacy wrack, bleached snow-white by the moon that rose in a clear unclouded patch. The meadow grass he had compared to a tapestry had since that earlier walk been cut and the land had become a pale stubbly desert. It was cold for the time of year. When he came to the river he saw that it was much swollen. In places the stones were totally submerged under the racing water.

Wexford whistled up the dog and stepped on briskly. He could see the bridge now, its stones gleaming silver

and the hart's tongue ferns between them like shivering
slivers of metal. Someone was standing on the parapet,
leaning over and looking down. It was some time before Wexford could decide whether it was a man or a
woman and when he realised it was a woman he called
out a brisk, cheerful good night so that she should not
be afraid.

'Good night, Chief Inspector.' The voice was low,
ironic, immediately identifiable. Wexford approached
Nora Fanshawe and she turned to face him.

'A fine evening after the storm,' he said. 'How's your
mother?'

'She'll live,' the girl said coolly. A reserve that was
part distaste blanked her features. Wexford knew that
look. He had seen it hundreds of times on the faces of
people who fancied that they had said too much to
him, opened their hearts too wide. Presumably they
imagined their confidences led him to regard them with
disgust or pity or contempt. If only they knew that to
him their revelations were but bricks in the house he
was trying to build, rungs on the ladder of discovery,
twisted curve-edged pieces in the current puzzle!

'Nothing fresh come back to her?'

'If you mean about the girl in the car, she says there
was no girl. I know when she's telling the truth.'

'People never remember what happened immediately
before they got hit on the head,' Wexford said cheerfully, 'especially when their skulls are fractured. It's a
medical fact.'

'Is that so? I mustn't keep you, Chief Inspector. Did
you know your dog's out in the road?'

Wexford retrieved Clytemnestra from the path of a
solitary oncoming car. The driver wound down his window and cursed him, adding that for two pins he'd tell
the police.

'Blooming thorn in my flesh, you are,' Wexford said
to the dog as he clipped the lead on. 'A source of humiliation.' He watched the girl retreat into the Olive
and Dove, the moonlight casting her shadow black,
straight and attenuated.

13

DETECTIVE CONSTABLE LORING was delighted at the
prospect of a day in London. He was mortally afraid of
Wexford who, he felt, treated him with a just but unremitting harshness. Someone had told Loring of the
chief inspector's almost paternal fondness for his prede-
cessor, Mark Drayton, and of his disillusionment when
Drayton had come to grief. It had been over some mess
with a girl and a bribe. Drayton, they told him, had
worn his hair long, had been surly and sarcastic and
clever and a devil with the women. Loring, therefore
had his own hair cropped eccentrically close and was as
eager, as bright and cheerful as he could be. Cleverness,
he felt, must come hereafter. At present he couldn't
compete with Wexford and Burden who were constant-
ly being clever all over the place. As for the women . . .
Loring was healthily keen. It afforded him considerable
pleasure to be going to London on a quest for three
missing girls. Wistfully he thought how very gratifying
it would be to find the right one and perhaps hear an
appreciative Wexford call him Peter. Drayton had fre-
quently been favoured by the use of his Christian name.

For all his dreams and his naïveté, Loring was a
perfectly competent officer. He made his mistakes and
he was frank about them. At twenty-one he was six
feet tall, as thin as he had been at fourteen, and desperately anxious for the day to come when he had finally
grown out of his acne. For all that—the spots were far
less noticeable than he believed—the girls he asked out
usually accepted his invitations and the older women he
interviewed patted their hair and smiled when he began

his questions. With luck, he sometimes thought, when he put on a bit of weight and got rid of those damned spots, he might one day look rather like John Neville. He was surprised and somewhat chagrined by his reception at the Eastcheap hairdresser's.

Carol Pearson was the girl whose disappearance he was investigating and he had already called on her mother in Muswell Hill. A skittish lady of forty with the mental age and taste in dress of eighteen, she had simpered over him and offered him gin. God knew, you were only young once—Mrs. Pearson looked as if she intended to be young several times over—and if Carol chose to pop off with her boy friend for a couple of months, she wasn't one to stand in her way. The boy friend was married, so what else could poor Carol do? The fact was she was sick to death of that job of hers, threatening to leave any time. Did Loring know the miserable wages they paid, the fact that the girls practically had to live on their tips? The boy friend had money. He was a travelling salesman, Mrs. Pearson said vaguely. But she couldn't recall his name, hadn't been able to tell the police when they asked before. Jack, Carol had called him. She never wrote letters. Easy come, easy go like her mother she was, and Mrs. Pearson gave him an ingratiating smile. She'd turn up one of these fine days.

So Loring had taken the tube to Tower Hill, getting lost a couple of times on the way. He walked up Eastcheap and picked out the office of the late Jerome Fanshawe by the brass plate on its marble doorway. Roma, the hairdresser's where Carol Pearson had worked, was diagonally opposite. Loring went in.

Never in his life had he seen anything like that receptionist. She wasn't the sort of girl you would dare to kiss, supposing you wanted to. Her hair was an artfully and deliberately tangled mass of red curls, the face beneath a miracle of paintwork, an artist's achievement of cream and amber light and shade with sooty eyes and blanked-out mouth. She wore a near-ankle-length black skirt, backless red boots and a short red caftan embroidered in gold.

Both her white telephones rang simultaneously as Loring entered. She lifted the receivers one after the other, said into each, 'Good morning. Roma. Will you hold the line one moment?' before resting them side by side on her enormous appointments book. 'Can I help you?'

Loring said he was a police officer and produced his card. She betrayed no surprise. 'One moment, please.' The telephone conversations were consecutively resumed, appointments made in the book. Loring glanced down the salon. Nothing like it had ever been seen in Kingsmarkham where clients still sat isolated in separate cells. Here the walls were lined in what looked like huge slices of pumpernickel. The chandeliers were black and silver mobiles and the floor a seemingly frozen lake of scarlet. Most of the assistants were men, tired worn-looking young men in light-weight suits drifted all over with many-coloured hair.

'If you've come about Carol Pearson,' the receptionist said contemptuously, 'you'll want Mr. Ponti. One moment, please.' The left-hand phone had rung again. 'Good morning. Roma. Will you hold the line a moment, please? He's in the gentleman's salon and he's styling so you can't . . . Just *one* moment.' She lifted the second phone. 'Good morning. Roma. Just one . . .'

'Thank you for all your help,' Loring said. He retreated into the street and entered the door to what he would have called the barber's. It was not very different from its Kingsmarkham equivalent. Things in the world of fashion evolve more slowly for men than for women.

Mr. Ponti looked more like a master at a public school than a hairdresser. He was tall and thin and he wore a perfectly plain, almost ascetic dark suit. The only indication that he had in fact been 'styling' was the handle of a pair of scissors protruding from his breast pocket and which Loring, so overpowering was the pedagogic impression, had at first taken for the rims of spectacles.

The other stylists leapt aside deferentially as he wove his way along the aisle between the chairs. The daylight from the door showed suntan powder on his cheekbones and now that he was close to, Loring saw him as an actor made up to play some academic part. The stoop was there, the vague though sharp expression, the myopic eyes.

A very faint trace of an Italian accent came through as he spoke. 'Carol?' he said. 'We have had the police here before and I told them, we cannot help.' He took the black leather handbag from Loring and fingered it appreciatively. 'This is very nice quality, very good.' With a shrug, he swept shut a concertina-style folding door that partly closed off the shop. 'Listen, she would not have this. I don't like to be cruel, but she was a cheap little girl. No style, no elegance. Ha!' From the interior of the bag he took out the Woolworth compact and the lipstick in its grazed metal case. 'These she might have, this cheap rubbish.' His long thin nose quivered distainfully.

Loring thought him an odious man. 'Have you ever had a Mr. Jerome Fanshawe among your clients?'

The name was evidently familiar. 'The stockbroker from across the street? I am told he is dead in a car accident.' Loring nodded. 'He has never been here.'

'Sure of that?'

'I never forget a client's name. All my clients are personally known to me.' Ponti snapped the bag shut and leant against the counter, looking bored.

'I'm wondering if Miss Pearson knew him,' Loring said, flinching from the scent of the man's after-shave. 'Did she ever mention him or did you ever see her go into his office?'

'I know nothing.' Ponti slid the door aside an inch and snapped his fingers. 'Those shots of Carol,' he called authoritatively, adding to Loring, 'I showed them to the other policemen. You may care to look at them.'

He fixed his pale brown eyes on Loring's own haircut and studied it reflectively and with faint distaste.

The photographs were pushed round the edge of the door and Loring took them. 'I used her once as a model,' said Ponti. 'She was no good, no damn' good at all.'

They looked all right to Loring. He had a simple taste in feminine beauty, demanding no more than that a girl should be pretty and fresh and smiling. For these shots Carol Pearson's hair had been dressed in fantastic pyramids of sausage curl, some of which spiralled to her shoulders. She looked ill-at-ease as if she wore instead of her own hair a Britannia helmet and she seemed to be shrinking beneath the weight, peering upwards with a nervous half-smile. Her eyes were painted ridiculously with diagonal lines radiating from the lower lids and her ear lobes dragged down by encrusted pendants. Under the *maquillage* she was a pretty girl, classically lovely, and Loring recalled sickeningly that it might be she who had come to her death, hideously disfigured, in blood and fire and water.

'No damn' good at all,' the hairdresser said again.

Doreen Dacres had turned up.

It was a curious story Loring heard from her married sister in Finchley. Doreen had gone to take up her club job in Eastbourne, arrived early and been kept waiting in a deserted lounge. There a well-informed cleaner had enlightened her as to what some of her new duties might consist of and Doreen, taking fright, had debunked into the street.

She had only five pounds in the world. Room and job in London having been abandoned, she took stock of her situation. The married sister had made it clear she wouldn't be welcome as a lodger with her and her husband, and their parents were in Glasgow, a city to which Doreen had sworn she would never return. Finally she had taken her luggage to a boarding house and, nervous that the club might catch up with her, booked herself in as Doreen Day and taken a shop assistant's job in the same name.

It was only when she wanted some clothes sent on that she had contacted her sister, six weeks later, by telephone. Thankfully, Loring crossed her off his list.

His last port of call was the Princess Louise Clinic in New Cavendish Street and he was directed by its porter to the nurses' home. This was a pleasant four-storey Regency house with white pillars flanking a bright blue front door liberally decorated with polished brass. A woman who called herself Home Sister came down to him and, before Loring could speak, she placed one pink finger against her lips.

'Quiet as a mouse, please. We mustn't forget the night staff are all getting their beauty sleep, must we?'

There was deep silence in the hall and a sweet scent far removed from the strong antiseptic of the hospital proper. It made Loring think of young girls, bevies of girls, whose freshly bathed bodies, as they passed through this place, left behind a mingled memory of Jasmine and Russian Leather and French Fern and New Mown Hay. He tip-toed after this stout navy-blue woman, who seemed to him half wardess and half mother superior, into a little lounge where there were chintz-covered chairs and flowers and an old television set.

'The girl who had the room next to Nurse Culross will be the best one to help you,' said Home Sister. 'Her name is Nurse Lewis, but of course it's out of the question that she should be disturbed if she's still sleeping.' She fixed him with a fierce censorious eye. 'Out of the question,' she said again. 'If you were the Home Secretary himself I wouldn't do it.' Apparently she was waiting for some show of defiance, and when Loring merely returned her look meekly, she lost some of her asperity and said, 'I'll make enquiries but I can't promise anything. Meanwhile, perhaps you'd care to look at some books.'

By this she meant magazines. The Princess Louise Nurses' Home was less sophisticated than Vigo's wait-

ing room and it offered instead of *Nova* and *Elle* the
Nursing Mirror and two copies of *Nursery World*
which Loring saw were fifteen years old. Left alone, he
stared out into the street.

An annexe to the clinic was a maternity hospital,
part of it but distinctly separate from the larger building. While he waited, Loring saw a Bentley draw up
and a young girl emerge leaning heavily on the arm of
her husband. Her body was huge and unwieldy and evidently she was already in labour. Ten minutes passed
and a Jaguar appeared. A similar little tableau took
place, but in this case the potential mother was older
and her maternity dress even more indicative of the
couturière from whom it had come. The Princess
Louise Clinic was busily fulfilling its function of re-
plenishing the upper classes.

It was nearly five o'clock before the door opened
slowly and Nurse Lewis came to him. Her eyes were
heavy and she looked as if she had just wakened. She
wore no make-up and she looked spotlessly clean, her
blouse stiff and crisp from the launderer, her pale, almost cream-fair hair damp and streaked where a
coarse-toothed comb had just passed through it.

'I'm sorry if I've kept you. I'm on nights you see.'

'That's all right,' Loring said. 'I work nights myself
sometimes. I know what it's like.'

Nurse Lewis sat down and her bare legs gleamed.
Her pink toes were like a little girl's in a little girl's
sandals.

'What did you want to know? I talked to the police
before.' She smiled earnestly. 'I told them all I knew
about Bridie Culross, but that wasn't much, you see.
Bridie didn't make close friends with girls, she was a
man's girl.'

'I'd like to hear anything you can tell me, Miss
Lewis.' Just let them talk. He had learnt that from
Wexford. 'About what sort of girl she was. She had a
lot of boy friends?'

'Well, this isn't a teaching hospital so there aren't

any medical students. She'd been here for a year since she qualified and she's been out with all the housemen.'

Loring wrote that down.

'The man she was most keen on—well, I never knew his name. She called him Jay.'

'As if it were an initial, do you mean? Like short for John or James or—Jerome?' 'I suppose so. I told the police all this before, you know. They weren't very interested.'

'You see, we don't usually bother very much about missing girls.'

'Why are you bothering now?'

'Let's leave that for a moment shall we, Miss Lewis? Tell me more about this Jay.'

She crossed her long bare legs. 'I never saw him,' she said. 'He was married, I'm afraid. Bridie didn't worry much about that sort of thing. Oh, and I remember her saying his wife had been a patient here.'

Charming, Loring thought. He visits his sick wife and picks up one of the nurses on his way out.

'I know what you're thinking,' said Nurse Lewis, 'and it wasn't very nice. He'd got lots of money and a nice car and all that. Bridie . . .' She hesitated and blushed. 'Well, Bridie lived with him actually.'

'Lived with him? In his house?'

'I didn't quite mean that.'

'Oh, I see.' Nurses, who ought to be used to the facts of life, were astonishingly prudish, he thought. 'Er—she went to spend a weekend with this man on Saturday, May 18th? In Brighton, wasn't it?'

'That's right, with Jay.' Nurse Lewis was still blushing at the implications of this weekend. 'She didn't come back. I heard Matron say she wouldn't have her back this time if she came.'

'She'd done it before, you mean?'

'Well, she'd been late a good many times and sometimes she didn't bother to come in after a late night. She said she wasn't going to dress operations and cart bedpans around for the rest of her life. She was going to have it soft. That's what she said. I thought she'd gone away with Jay to live with him properly. Well, not properly, but you know what I mean.'

'Tell me, did he give her presents? Did she have a very good black handbag with a Mappin and Webb label? This one?'

'Oh, yes! He gave it to her for her birthday. She was twenty-two. Look . . .' She frowned and leant towards him. 'What is this? You've found her handbag but you haven't found her?'

'We're not sure yet,' said Loring, but he was.

Wexford would be displeased if he went back with just this and no more. Loring would have liked another day in London, but it was hardly worth facing Wexford's rage, the necessary preliminary to granting it. He went into the main hospital building and rang the bell at the enquiry desk. While he waited he looked about him, reflecting that he had never been in a hospital like this one before. His impression was that he was the first person to enter it for a long time with less than five thousand a year and he thought of Stowerton Infirmary where the outpatients sat for hours on hard chairs, where the paint was peeling off the walls and where everyone seemed to be in a hurry.

Here, instead, was an atmosphere of lazy graciousness as in a large private house. A very faint odour of disinfectant was almost entirely masked by the scent of flowers, sweet peas in copper jugs and, on the enquiry desk, a single rose in a fluted glass. The floor was carpeted in dark red Wilton.

Loring glanced up the branched staircase and watched the receptionist descend. He asked for a list of all the patients who had entered the Princess Louise Clinic in the past year and his request was received with a look of outrage.

It took him nearly half an hour, during which he was passed from one official personage to another, before he got the permission he wanted.

The list was long and imposing. Loring had never seen *Debrett* but he felt that this catalogue might have been a section of it. Nearly half the names on it were preceded by a title and among the plain Misters he recognized a distinguished industrialist, a former cabinet minister and a television personality who was a household word. Among the women was a duchess, a ballet dancer, a famous model. Loring couldn't find Dorothy Fanshawe. He searched all through the list again because he had been so certain her name would be there. It wasn't there.

J for Jerome, but J also for John, James, Jeremy, Jonathan, Joseph. Was Bridget Culross's lover the husband of the Hon. Mrs. John Frazer-Bennet of Wilton Crescent or the husband of Lady James Fyne of The Boltons? Loring concluded and supposed Wexford would also conclude him to be the late husband of Dorothy Fanshawe.

14

THE YOUNG PERTWEES were honeymooning in Jack's father's house. Their own flat wouldn't be ready for a fortnight and Jack had cancelled the hotel booking. There was nowhere else for them to go and nothing much to do. Jack had taken his annual holiday, so here he was at home. Where else would he be? It was, after all, the only honeymoon he would ever get. Usually in his spare time he did a bit of painting or decorating or went to the dogs or down the Dragon. Marilyn made her dresses and giggled with her girl friends and went to meetings calculated to stir up social strife. These are not occupations for a honeymoon and the young Pertwees felt that to follow their old ways during this period, provided as it were for festive idleness and the

indulgence of love, would be a kind of desecration. As
Jack put it, you can't stay in bed all day, so they spent
most of the time sitting hand in hand in the little-used
parlour. Marilyn was only articulate on the subject of
politics and Jack was never talkative. Neither of them
ever read a book and they were abysmally bored. Each
would have died rather than confess this to the other
and they knew in their hearts that their silence was no
threat of future discord. Everything would be fine once
Jack was back at work and they were in their own flat.
When there were his workmates to discuss and the furniture and having her mother to tea. Now they filled
their silences with sad reflections on Charlie Hatton
and although this too was no subject for a honeymoon, their shared memory of him expressed in hackneyed and sentimental phrases passed the time away
and, because it was selfless and sincere, strengthened
their love.

It was thus that Wexford found them.

Marilyn let him into the house, her only greeting a
shrug. He too could be laconic and brusque and when
Jack rose clumsily to his feet, Wexford said only, 'I've
come to talk to you about McCloy.'

'You talk then. You tell me.'

The girl smiled at that. 'Give us a cig, Jack,' she
said, and she gave her husband a fond proud look.
'Yes,' she said, coming up close to Wexford, 'you give
us a lecture. We'd like to know, wouldn't we, Jack? We
don't mind listening, we've nothing else to do.'

'That doesn't sound too good on your honeymoon.'

'Some honeymoon,' Jack grumbled. 'You think this
is the way I'd planned it?'

Wexford sat down and faced them. 'I didn't kill
Charlie Hatton,' he said. 'I didn't even know him. You
did. You were supposed to be his friend. You've got
a funny way of showing it.'

A spasm of pain shivered the red from Jack's face.
He took his wife's hand and he sighed. 'He's dead. You
can't be friends with a dead man. All you've got is his
memory to hold on to.'

'Give me a piece of your memory, Mr. Pertwee.'

Jack looked him full in the face and now the blood returned, beating under the skin. 'You're always playing with words, twisting, being clever . . .'

His wife cut in, 'Showing your bloody education!'

'Leave it, love I feel the same, but it's no good. It's . . . You've made up your mind Charlie was a crook, haven't you? It wouldn't be no good me telling you what he was really like, generous, good-hearted, never let you down. But it wouldn't be no good, would it?'

'I doubt if it would help me to find who killed him.'

'He found us our flat,' Jack said. 'D'you know what he did? The bloke that's got it now, he wanted key money. Two hundred he wanted and Charlie put that up. On loan, of course, but he wouldn't take no interest. May the 21st it was. I'll never forget that date as long as I live. Charlie'd been driving all the day before, driving down from the north. But he come here in the morning to say he'd found this flat for us. I was at work but Marilyn got a couple of hours off from the shop and went down there with him. Promised the bloke the money, he did, more like he was her dad than—just a friend.'

May the 21st. The day Hatton had ordered his teeth. Just after the robbery that never was. Here was another example of what Hatton had done with the small fortune he had somehow got out of McCloy.

'I'll let you have it whenever you want, Charlie said. Just say the word. You should have seen him when we did say the word! I reckon giving things away made him really happy.'

'This place,' said Marilyn, mildly for her, 'well, it's not the same without Charlie Hatton and that's a fact.'

Sentimental twaddle, Wexford thought harshly. 'Where did he get all his money, Mrs. Pertwee?'

'I could ask him that, could I? I could just come out with it like that? I may be common working class but I was brought up right. I've got manners. So, for God's sake, leave me out of it.'

'Mr. Pertwee?'

He would have to answer, Wexford thought. He had said too much and been too self-controlled to plead distress as an excuse this time. Jack put his fist up to his forehead and leant on his elbow.

'Where did he get it? Two hundred and fifty pounds for his teeth, two hundred for you . . .' How it mounted up! 'Money for his furniture, his wife's clothes, your wedding present, money going week by week into the bank. He was earning twenty pounds a week, Mr. Pertwee. What do you earn?'

'Mind your own damn' business.'

'Come on now, love,' said Pertwee miserably. He looked at Wexford, biting his lip. 'Bit more than that,' he said. 'Bit more in a good week.'

'Could you lend your best friend two hundred pounds?'

'My best friend's dead!'

'Don't stall, please.' Wexford said sharply. 'You knew what Hatton's life was, Pertwee. Don't tell me you never asked yourself where all that money came from. You asked yourself and you asked him. How did Hatton get to be a rich man on May 21st?'

And now Pertwee's brow cleared. He sighed and there was a tiny gleam of triumph in his eyes. 'I don't know. You could ask me from now till Doomsday. I can't tell you because I don't know.' He hesitated. 'You asked me about McCloy,' he said. 'Charlie didn't get no money from McCloy on May 21st. He couldn't have.'

Then Wexford questioned him and probed and used all the subtlety years of experience had given him. Pertwee held his wife's hand, shook his head, answered monosyllabically and at last he dried up.

At the special court held to give his case its preliminary hearing, Maurice Cullam pleaded guilty to stealing one hundred and twenty pounds from the dead body of Charlie Hatton and was remanded in custody.

Further charges might be preferred against him, Burden intimated.

He didn't believe Cullam was a murderer. His house had been searched from top to bottom but no money had been found. Cullam had no bank account and no more than a few shillings in the Post Office. The only effect of the search was the incidental discovery of such savage bruises on the legs of Samantha Cullam as to necessitate her removal into the care of the county authority. Further charges would be preferred against her father, but they would not be in the nature of murder or larceny.

'What's your next step?' said Dr. Crocker idly, on his way back from examining the little girl's injuries. 'A bastard who's beat up a kid like that wouldn't stop at murder, if you ask me.'

'It doesn't follow.'

'The trouble with you lot you're always looking for complications. Here's the boss now. I've just been asking Mike here if you've got a vacancy for me on your staff, seeing how I've helped you with your enquiries.'

Wexford gave him a sour look. 'Cullam's no killer.'

'Maybe not. Prefers his victims undersized and female,' and the doctor launched into a heated tirade against the arrested man.

'Oh, I'm sick of the whole bloody thing,' Wexford shouted suddenly. 'I've spent the entire morning trying to pump Pertwee. Sentimental fool! Everyone knows Hatton was a thief and a twister, but Pertwee won't talk because he doesn't want to sully the fellow's memory.'

'It's not a bad principle,' said Burden.

'Any principle's bad, Mike, if putting it into practice means a murderer goes free. Hatton did jobs for McCloy and one weekend in May he started squeezing his old employer. He squeezed him pretty hard, I can tell you. Two hundred pounds for Pertwee, two hundred and fifty for Vigo .... Oh, I can't go into it all again.'

'So you're giving up?' said the doctor.

Burden looked deeply shocked and he clicked his tongue old-maidishly. But Wexford said calmly, 'I'm going to try another line for the present and I'm relying on you to smooth the path. You're supposed to be a doctor, after all.'

Mrs. Fanshawe was alone when they got back to the Infirmary, but she was out of bed. Wrapped in a black nylon négligé—afterwards Crocker called it a *peignoir*—she was sitting in an armchair reading *Fanny Hill*.

'A chief inspector and an inspector and a doctor to see you,' said Nurse Rose. Mrs. Fanshawe tucked *Fanny Hill* under her new copy of *Homes and Gardens*. She knew now that Nurse Rose was a nurse and not a maid and that she was in hospital. But that was no reason why the girl should take the attitude that her patient was honoured by this visit. Mrs. Fanshawe knew what was due to her. Besides, she was glowing with the self-confidence of someone who, having been distressingly and obtusely disbelieved for days, has now proved her point. Nora was alive; Nora was here, or at least, a couple of miles away in Kingsmarkham. Probably this deputation, sent from whatever authority it was that had stupidly persisted in burying her, had been sent to apologise.

Hastily Mrs. Fanshawe grabbed a handful of rings from the jewel case her sister had brought in and it was a lavishly decorated hand that she extended graciously to Wexford.

Wexford saw a discontented face with sagging chin muscles and lines pulling the mouth down at the corners. Mrs. Fanshawe's eyes were hard and bright and her voice acid when she said:

'I'm not mad, you see. Everyone thought I was insane when I said my daughter was alive. Now, I expect, they'd like to apologise.'

'Certainly, Mrs. Fanshawe. We all apologise.' Apologies cost nothing. He smiled blandly into the petulant face and suddenly he remembered what this woman's

daughter had told him. How her father had paid her
mother to let him have his women in the house. 'No
one thought you were mad,' he said, 'but you'd been in
a serious accident.' She nodded smugly and Wexford
thought, She's no madder than she's ever been. But
what did that amount to? She had never, he considered,
been very bright.

Nurse Rose scampered in with two more chairs and
she bridled, giggling a little, when all three men
thanked her effusively.

'You can get me another cushion,' said Mrs. Fanshawe. 'No, not a pillow, a proper cushion. And then
you can ring my daughter.'

'In ten minutes, Mrs. Fanshawe,' said Nurse Rose,
tired but bright as ever.

'Just as you like.' Mrs. Fanshawe waited until she
was gone and then she said pettishly, 'This is supposed
to be a private room, not that anyone would think so
the cavalier treatment you get. Half the time you ring
the bell they don't come.'

Wexford said dryly, 'You don't find it as comfortable
as the Princess Louise Clinic?'

'What's that supposed to mean?'

'I understand you were in the Princess Louise Clinic
in Cavendish Street in London last year.'

'You understood wrong then. The only time I've
ever been in hospital was when my daughter was born.'
She sighed impatiently when the door opened and
Nurse Rose entered with tea for four. 'I thought you
were under-staffed? These gentlemen are officials. They
aren't paying a social call.'

But Dr. Crocker said, 'Thank you very much, my
dear,' and he ogled Nurse Rose outragiously. 'Will you
be mother, Mrs. Fanshawe, do the honours?'

The rings clinked as she poured the tea. She eyed
him suspiciously. 'Well, my daughter's alive,' she said,
'and I've never been to the Princess Louise Clinic. What
else d'you want?'

Wexford just glanced at Burden and Burden said,
'Your daughter's alive but there was a dead girl lying

by the wreckage of your car. Any idea who she could be? The name Bridget Culross mean anything to you?'

'Nothing at all.'

'She was a nurse.' Mrs. Fanshawe's sniff told him eloquently what she thought of nurses. 'She was twenty-two and a girl who might be she was dead in the road with your husband.'

'She was never alive in the car with my husband.'

'Mrs. Fanshawe,' Wexford said carefully, 'are you quite sure you gave no one a lift from Eastbourne, from Eastover?'

'I am sick of this,' said Dorothy Fanshawe. 'I don't know how many times I've told you. There was no one else in the car.'

He looked at her and he thought, *Would* you tell me? Are you ashamed that your husband flaunted these women at you, paid you? Or is it that you don't care any more, haven't cared for years, and there really was no one in the car?

Dorothy Fanshawe watched her rings winking in the sunlight. She avoided meeting the eyes of these tiresome men. They thought her stupid or a liar. She knew very well what they were getting at. Nora had been talking to them. Nora hadn't the decency and the discretion to keep silent about Jerome's nasty habits.

How stupid these men were! Their faces were all embarrassed and prudish. Did they really suppose she cared what Jerome had done? Jerome was dead and buried deep. Good riddance. All the money was hers and Nora's now, more money than all those foolish-looking men would earn between the lot of them in their lifetimes. As long as Nora didn't do anything stupid like marrying that Michael, there was nothing in the world to worry about.

Dorothy Fanshawe drank her tea and put the cup down with a sharp tap. Then she rang the bell and as the door opened, said:

'We shall want some more hot water.'

She had been going to say please, but she cut the word off and swallowed it. Suddenly Nurse Rose, so plump and pink and young, had looked just like that maid Jerome used to paw about when she was making the beds. She smiled a little, though, for Jerome was dead and there were no maids or nurses or soft young flesh where he had gone.

'Exhumation!' Burden exclaimed. 'You couldn't do it.'

'Well, I could, Mike,' said Wexford mildly. 'I daresay we could get an order. Only she's been dead so long and the face was in a mess then and ... God, I could wring Camb's bloody neck!'

'The aunt was so sure,' Burden said.

'We'd best get that Lewis girl down from the Princess Louise Clinic, show her the clothes. But if the girl was Bridget Culross, what was she doing in Fanshawe's car with Fanshawe's wife?'

'I believe Mrs. Fanshawe, sir.'

'So do I, Mike. So do I.' Wexford said it again to convince himself. 'I think Fanshawe was capable of taking the girl to his bungalow and sleeping with her while his wife was there. I believe Mrs. Fanshawe would have stood it. As to the girl—well, we don't know enough about her to say. But Nora Fanshawe knew nothing of it and Nora Fanshawe was with them until the Saturday. They thought she was going to stay on. So where does Culross come in? And where was she stowed away on the Friday night?'

'It's very disgraceful,' said Burden and he made a face like someone who has been shown a disgusting mess of offal.

'Never mind that. Leave the ethics and concentrate on the circumstantial evidence. The more I hear of them the more I go back to my old idea.'

'Which is?'

'In the light of our fresh information, this: Bridget Culross never knew Fanshawe. His wife was never a patient at the Princess Louise Clinic, therefore he isn't Jay. Probably she went to Eastbourne or Brighton with Jay, rowed with him and tried to get back to London on her own. Maybe she hitch-hiked. A lorry driver put her down on the Stowerton By-pass, she thumbed a lift from Fanshawe—maybe she stepped out into the road, he couldn't stop, hit her head and crashed. How's that?'

Burden looked dubious. 'That means to thumb her lift she would have had to be standing on the soft verge between the two carriageways.'

'And any normal hitch-hiker stands on the nearside and waits for someone coming down the slow lane?'

'Mm-hm. On the other hand we do know that Mrs. Fanshawe heard her husband call out "God!" just before the crash; in fact, that was the last thing he ever did say.'

'I hope,' said Wexford, 'the cry was heard by Providence and interpreted as a plea for forgiveness.' He chuckled sourly. 'So he sees the girl standing on the road, cries out, swerves, hits her. Why did she have only a little loose change in her handbag, no keys, nothing to identify her? Why would a lorry driver put her down on the by-pass instead of in the town?'

'It's your theory, sir.'

'I know it is, damn it!' said Wexford.

But he kept thinking about that lorry driver. Charlie Hatton had passed that way a quarter of an hour before the accident. He couldn't have seen the accident. Could he have seen the girl waiting to thumb a lift? Or could he have been the driver who had left her there? The trouble was Charlie Hatton had been driving in the other direction.

It had been May 20th and on May 21st Charlie Hatton was a rich man. There must be a connection. But where did McCloy come into all this?

Every police force in England and Wales was now looking for Alexander James McCloy, light brown hair, medium height, aged 42, late of Moat Hall, near Stamford in Lincolnshire; because of Burden's recent discoveries; they were looking for him in Scotland too.

This time it was Mr. Pertwee senior who admitted him into the house. Still hand-in-hand the honeymooners were watching television.

'Christ, do we have to?' Marilyn said crossly when her husband got up and switched off the party political broadcast. 'What d'you want this time?'

Wexford said, 'In November of last year your friend Hatton arranged to have the lorry he drove for his employer Mr. Bardsley hi-jacked. When I say arranged, I mean he did so under the instructions of his other employer, Alexander James McCloy. Hatton got a little tap on the head and they tied him up, just to make things look more realistic. Fortunately, Mr. Bardsley was insured. He wasn't, though, when it happened again in March. That time he had to stand the loss himself, unaware, of course, that a good percentage of it was finding its way directly into Hatton's pocket.'

He stopped and looked into Jack Pertwee's pale face. Jack returned his stare for an instant and then dipped his face down into his hands.

'Don't you admit nothing, Jack,' said Marilyn fiercely.

'On the 19th of May,' Wexford continued, 'Hatton drove up to Leeds. He'd been ill and he took it slowly, returning on the next day, Monday, May 20th. While he was in Leeds or on the road he encountered McCloy. He encountered him or discovered something about him to McCloy's disadvantage. Enough, anyway, to put him into a position from which he was able to blackmail McCloy to the extent of several pounds.'

'It's a filthy lie,' said Jack in a choking voice.

'Very well, Mr. Pertwee. I'd like you to come down to the police station with me, if you please . . .'

'But he's just got married!' interrupted the father.

'Mrs. Pertwee may accompany him if she chooses. The situation has arisen that information is being deliberately withheld in a murder enquiry. Are you ready, Mr. Pertwee?'

Jack didn't move. Then the hands that clutched his forehead began to tremble. Marilyn put her arms around him protectively, but not gently, and her lips twisted as if she would have liked to spit in Wexford's face.

'Blackmail?' Jack stammered. 'Charlie?' He took his hands away and Wexford saw that he was weeping. 'That's crazy!'

'I don't think so, Mr. Pertwee.'

'He couldn't have,' Jack said, mouthing something Wexford didn't quite catch.

'What did you say?'

'I said, he couldn't have. McCloy's inside. You're a copper, aren't you? You know what I mean. McCloy's in prison.'

15

THE NEWS FROM Scotland came through at almost exactly the same time as Jack Pertwee's revelation. Alexander McCloy had been sent to prison for two years on April 23rd, having been found guilty with two other men of organising a break-in at a supermarket in Dundee on early-closing day, and stealing goods to the value of twelve hundred pounds. A caretaker had been slightly injured during the course of the robbery and McCloy would have received a heavier sentence but for his unblemished record.

'So while Hatton was in Leeds that May weekend,' said Wexford in the morning, 'McCloy had already been safely locked up in Scotland for a month.'

'It looks that way,' said Burden.

'And that not only means he wasn't available to be blackmailed, but also that Hatton's source of—well, I was nearly going to say legitimate, income was cut off.

In fact, in May Hatton found himself shorter of money than probably at any time since he was married.'

'Mrs. Hatton said that when he was ill during the previous week he hesitated about sending for the doctor privately. By that time he'd presumably spent whatever he'd made when they nicked Bardsley's lorry in March.'

'At his rate of expenditure,' Wexford cut in, 'he probably had. It must have given him quite a nasty feeling. Panicked him, I daresay. Can't you imagine him, Mike, looking to the future when he wouldn't be able to stand all those rounds in the Dragon or take his wife frittering on a Saturday afternoon or cut a fine open-handed figure at his friend's wedding?'

'I imagine he quickly looked round for another source of supply.'

'We'll go up to the Stowerton By-pass,' Wexford said, getting up, 'and do some reconnoitring. Our two cases are converging. Mike, and unless I'm mistaken, they're soon going to bump.'

'There was no suitcase,' said Sergeant Martin, 'but I want you to look at the clothes she was wearing. They're in a bad way, Miss Lewis. You must try to keep calm.'

She was a nurse and trained to control herself. Martin took her into another room where the burnt torn clothes lay like rubbish heap rags on the table. Each blackened tattered garment lay separate from the others and there was something in this arrangement that suggested a parody of a draper's window.

The bodice of the coat and of the dress were charred fragments, although their skirts were almost intact and patches of orange and yellow showed between the scorch marks. The dead girl's brassière was an ellipse of wire from which every shred of cotton and lace had been burnt away. Margaret Lewis shuddered, keeping her hands behind her back. Then she touched the orange shoes, the white lace stockings as wide-meshed and fine as a hair-net, and she began to cry.

'I gave her those stockings,' she whispered, 'for her birthday.'

Their tops only were charred, but a long brown mark ran down to the knee of one of them where a flame had licked. Martin put his arm under the girl's elbow and led her away.

'I'll tell you everything I can about Bridie,' she said and she gulped the tea Loring had brought her. 'And everything she told me about Jay. She met him in October while she was nursing his wife. The wife was in a long time on account of having a threatened toxaemia and Bridie used to go out with him after he'd visited her. She'd come off duty at eight-thirty, you see, and he'd just about be leaving.

'Well, he dropped her after his wife left the clinic and I thought that was the end of it. But it wasn't. He turned up again in May and the whole thing was on again. Bridie started talking about marrying him. Oh, it was awful, really, and I didn't used to listen much. I wish I had now.'

'Did you ever see him, Miss Lewis?' Martin asked.

Margaret Lewis shook her head. The colour had come back into her cheeks and she wore no make-up to smear when she dabbed at the lids with a spotless handkerchief. 'We weren't working in the same department, you see. Lots of people must have. You'll have to ask the other girls. Bridie said he was quite old, lots older than her, and that was the one thing that made her—well, hesitate, if you know what I mean.'

'So you wouldn't know if this is him?' And Martin showed her a photograph of Jerome Fanshawe. It had been taken by flash at a company dinner and the face was hard, confident, heavily jowled, but because of its arrogance and its strength and despite its age, not unattractive to women.

She looked at it with the distaste of the very young and, not answering him, said, 'I told you they went to Brighton on the 18th of May?' Loring nodded. 'Bridie was going to be met by him at Marble Arch. I saw her go off in that yellow coat and dress. She said she'd have to amuse herself during the daytime because Jay would be at his conference. That's why he was going, you see, to be at this conference.'

Loring gave another encouraging smile. This was the sort of thing Wexford wanted. Then he remembered his search through the clinic's patient list.

'The man we had in mind,' he said carefully, 'we couldn't find his name among the clinic's patients, you know. His wife denies she was ever in there.'

The girl touched the photograph and looked up at him in bewilderment. 'How old is she, for goodness' sake?'

'The wife? Fifty, fifty-five.'

'I'm sorry,' Margaret Lewis blushed. 'I think this has been my fault. Jay's wife was in the *maternity* department. They're always separate, you know, the general and the maternity departments in hospitals. Always. Bridie had done her midwifery and she was nursing Jay's wife when she was ill before the birth and while she was having the baby.'

Burden was driving. With the accident plan Camb had given him on his lap, Wexford looked up and said:

'Park in the next lay-by, Mike, and we'll walk.'

An ancient milestone which had always stood on the bank since this highway was the coaching road to London, by chance pin-pointed the crash spot. From it a slow incline wound down into the valley.

The northbound and southbound sections of the by-pass, opened a year before, were separated by a strip of grass on which grew clumps of thin birch trees. Fanshawe's Jaguar had struck one of these trees, overturned and caught fire. Wexford and Burden waited for two cars and a van to pass and then they crossed the road to the centre strip.

A large area of this grass had been burnt but by now new growth had replaced it and there was nothing but a ragged black stump to show where the crash tree had been.

'First,' said Wexford, 'we'll work on the assumption that the girl was in the car with the Fanshawes, she was Jerome Fanshawe's fancy piece and he was driving her back to London. Who sits where? Mrs. Fanshawe in the back and her supplanter next to Don Juan or vice versa?'

'Surely there must have been some amount of pretence, sir,' said Burden, wrinkling his fastidious nose. 'It can't have been all open and above-board. The girl would have sat in the back.'

'It's the seat on the driver's left that's called the suicide seat, Mike, and whereas the girl died, Mrs. Fanshawe is still alive. If the girl was there at all, she sat in the front.' Wexford made a sweeping gesture with his right hand. 'Up comes Fanshawe, driving like the maniac he was at eighty or so. Now there's no evidence of a burst tyre and the windscreen didn't shatter. What did Fanshawe see that made him cry out "God!" and pull the wheel over?'

'Something in the road?'

'Yes, but what? A big piece of metal or a wooden box? He'd have sailed right over cardboard. Anyway, they didn't find anything in the road afterwards.'

'A dog?'

'Fanshawe wouldn't have crashed for the sake of a dog. And he didn't hit one because there was no body.'

'Then he saw the girl herself,' said Burden carefully, 'stepping out of the centre section to wave him down.'

'But we're assuming the girl was *in* the car. Don't you agree with me now that she can't have been?'

Burden walked a little way away from him and stopped by the black birch stump. 'If the girl stepped off here,' he said, taking a couple of paces towards the fast lane, 'and Fanshawe thought he was going to hit her, why didn't he swerve the *left*, into the middle lane, instead of to the right? The road must have been clear as there were no witnesses to the accident. He swerved inwards, to the right, mounted this centre strip and hit the tree.'

Wexford shrugged. A car in the fast lane leapt past

them at seventy. 'Feel like experimenting, Mike?' he said with a grin. 'Just pop out into the road now, wave your arms and see what happens.'

'You can, if you're so keen,' said Burden, involuntarily retreating from the edge. 'I want to stay alive.'

'Funny that girl didn't. Mike, it couldn't have been straight suicide, could it?'

Burden said thoughtfully, 'I suppose it could have at that. Assume she has no connection with Fanshawe, assume she went to the South Coast with another boy friend who ditched her so that she had to hitch a lift as far as here. The driver that brought her to this point might then have dropped her at her own request. She crosses to the centre section, waits until a fast car comes and steps out suddenly in front of it. Of course, that doesn't explain why Fanshawe pulled to the right instead of to the left.'

'And it doesn't explain why everything that might have identified her was *removed* from her handbag. If she was a suicide, there's no possible reason why she should have removed it herself. Anyway, you seem to have forgotten our main reason for coming here. The crash occurred at ten to ten and Hatton passed on the other highway, going in the other direction, at approximately twenty to. Impoverished Hatton, desperate to replenish the empty coffers. Suppose he passed a little later than that and saw the girl step out? Now, if Fanshawe were still alive, if, say, he'd killed the girl without damage to his car, and had simply driven on, Hatton might have blackmailed him. But Fanshawe is dead, Mike.'

Now it was Burden's turn to shrug and look baffled. He eyed the other highway, the southbound section, the hedge that bounded it, the meadows behind that hedge. The road came to a crest some fifty yards to the north of where they stood and above this ridge nothing but the pale milky sky was visible.

'If there was some sort of foul play,' he said thoughtfully, 'if, for instance, the girl was pushed into the road ... Oh, I know it's fantastic, but haven't you got some-

thing of the sort in mind yourself? If she was pushed
and Hatton, approaching over the brow of that hill,
was a witness, why didn't whoever it was doing the
pushing, see him first? His lorry was an outsize very
high van and anyone standing here would see the top
of it appearing over the crest seconds before its driver
could see him. Look, here comes a lorry now.'

Wexford turned his eyes towards the brow of the
hill. The lorry's roof loomed above it and it seemed
that some seconds passed before the cab came into
view.

'It was dark,' he said.

'Anyone standing where we are could see its head-
lights at precisely the same time as its driver saw him.'

The same thought striking each man simultaneously,
they walked towards the crest. Beneath them half Sussex lay spread, broad meadows, green and gold, the
dense bluish shadows of woodland and in the folds between, farmhouses and the occasional pointing spire of
a church. Through this pastoral landscape the road
wound its twin white ribbon, hummocking here, dip-
ping there, and sometimes entirely concealed by the
green swelling land.

Not more than twenty yards beyond the crest, the
southbound section widened into an arc and in this
lay-by the occupants of two cars sat picnicking.

'Perhaps he parked here for a bit,' Burden said.
'Walked up this way for—well, a natural purpose or
just because he needed air. He hadn't been well, after
all.'

But Wexford looked at the view and said presently,
'Where every prospect pleases, and only man is vile.'

The huge American car with its splayed fins dwarfed
every other vehicle in the Olive's car park. Crossing the
forecourt with Burden, Wexford saw on closer scrutiny
that it was neither new nor well cared for. One of its
headlamps was broken and its chrome rim showed that
it had been broken a long time. Scratches marred the
bluish-green finish on its wings. Here in this tiny car

park in a small country town it was an unwieldy mass of metal that doubtless gave a poor return for the petrol it devoured. It took up an immense amount of space but its seating capacity was small.

'Reminds me of one of those prehistoric monsters,' said Wexford, 'all brawn and no brain.'

'Must have been grand once, though.'

'That's what they said about the dinosaurs.'

They sat in the saloon bar. In the far corner Nora Fanshawe sat on a leather settle beside a huge fair man with a small head. His expression was vapid, his shoulders of Mister Universe proportions. Another dinosaur, Wexford thought, and suddenly he was sure this was the owner of the car.

'We keep running into each other, Miss Fanshawe.'

'You keep running into me,' said the girl dryly. She wore another of her finely tailored, neatly stitched suits, navy blue this time and as slick and business-like as a uniform. 'This is Michael Jameson. You may remember, I mentioned him to you.'

The hand that took Wexford's had a damp palm. 'Nice little place this, if a bit off the map.'

'Depends where you make your maps.'

'Come again? Oh, I see. Ha ha!'

'We were just going,' said Nora Fanshawe. Then her strong masculine voice quavered a little as she said, 'Ready, Michael?' Suddenly she was vulnerable. Wexford knew that wistful pleading look. He had seen it before in the eyes of plain women, the pathetic terror of rejection that, because it deprives them of confidence, makes them plainer.

Jameson got up sluggishly, reluctantly; he winked at Wexford and that wink was as eloquent as words.

'Off to see your mother, Miss Fanshawe?'

The girl nodded and Jameson said, 'The old girl keeps her on her toes.'

'Let's go, Michael.' She linked her arm in his and held it tight. Wexford watched them go, telling himself he was a fool to let the scene upset him. She was gruff, rude, unfeminine. She was also peculiarly honest and she lacked the talent of self-deception. Not for a moment did Wexford doubt that she knew this man was quite unworthy of her, in intelligence, in probity, in character. But he was good looking and she had money.

'A bit of an oaf,' said Burden.

Wexford lifted the curtain and between the fuchsias he saw Jameson get into the huge car and start the engine. Nora Fanshawe was not the kind of woman who looks on courtesy from men as her right. The car was already in motion before she got herself into the passenger seat. Jameson had not even opened the door for her from the inside.

16

'I WANT YOU all to concentrate,' Wexford said. 'Don't tell me it was a long time ago and you can't remember. It was only about seven weeks ago. You'll be surprised what you can remember if you try.'

They were sitting in Lilian Hatton's flat, Wexford confronting the three people on the sofa. Mrs. Hatton wore a black cotton frock and all the jewellery Charlie had ever given her. Her face was white and tense, still stained by the tears she had shed when Wexford had revealed her husband's source of income. Was it a revelation or had she always known? Wexford couldn't make his mind up about that. For all her short skirt and her make-up and the equipment in her kitchen, she was essentially at heart a Victorian wife, helpless, clinging, accepting all her husband's quirks with un-questioning passivity. She would no more have asked Charlie if the brooch she wore was bought with ill-gotten money than her nineteenth-century counterpart would have asked her lord and master to admit that his presents to her were the result of cheating at cards. Hers not to reason why, hers but to accept and praise and adore. Now, as he faced her, Wexford wondered how this anachronism would fend for herself in the world Charlie called a battlefield.

'He always talked about fighting for what you wanted,' she had said wretchedly, 'about being one up on the next man. Planning his—his stra . . . His stra—something.'

'Strategy?'

'That's it. Like as if he was a general.'

A soldier of fortune, Wexford thought, a mercenary.

The other two knew all right, the young Pertwees. They had finally admitted as much and now Marilyn said sullenly, 'He was getting back at the big nobs. What does losing a load mean to them? They're all robbers, anyway. Capitalism's organised robbery of the working classes. Charlie was only taking back what was due to him.'

'Having his revenge on society perhaps, Mrs. Pertwee?'

'Yeah, and why not? When we've got a real people's government in this country, folks like Charlie'll get their fair shares and there won't be no crime. Or what you call crime. When we get real socialism.'

'Charlie always voted Conservative,' said Lilian Hatton. 'I don't know, Marilyn, I don't think . . .'

Wexford interrupted them. There was no room for laughter in this flat, yet he wanted to laugh. 'Let's postpone the political discussion, shall we? Mrs. Hatton, you've had time to think now and I want you to tell me all you remember about your husband's departure for Leeds on Sunday, May 19th and his return on the 20th.'

She cleared her throat and glanced hesitantly at Jack Pertwee, waiting perhaps for more masculine directions and more masculine support.

'Don't you worry, Lily,' said Marilyn, 'I'm here.'

'I'm sure I don't know what I'd do without you.

Well . . . Well, Charlie'd been ill and I didn't want him
to go but he would insist.'

'Was he worried about money, Mrs. Hatton?'

'Charlie never bothered me with things like that. Oh,
wait a minute though . . . He did say the doctor would
have to wait to get paid. I remember him saying that.
D'you want me to go on about that Sunday?' Wexford
nodded. 'Jack and Marilyn came in the evening for a
three-handed solo.'

'That's right,' said Marilyn, 'and Charlie rung you
from Leeds while we was here.'

Mrs. Hatton looked at her admiringly. 'So he did.
Yes, he did.'

'What did he say to you?'

'Nothing much. It was mostly—well, asking me how
I was and saying he missed me.' She sniffed and bit her
lip. 'We didn't like being separated. We couldn't sleep
away from each other.'

'More like sweethearts than man and wife they
were,' said Jack and he put his arm around her shoulders.

'Did he say he was still feeling unwell?'

'Bit under the weather. He'd have come back that
night else.'

'Did he sound pleased, excited?'

'Down in the dumps, if anything.'

'Now I want you to be very exact about this. Precisely what time did your husband come home on the
following night, the Monday night?'

She didn't hesitate. 'Ten on the dot. He'd said ten
the night before and I'd made him a chicken casserole.
Charlie'd bought me a kitchen timer back in March,
but it went wrong and had to go back to the shop, and
that was the first time I'd used it. I set it for ten and it
just started pinging when Charlie put his key in the
door.'

'How was he when he came in?'

'In himself, d'you mean? He'd had his sickness back,
he said, and he'd had to stop a couple of times on the
road. He'd have been back earlier if he hadn't stopped.

He wanted to get back earlier, you see, to surprise me.' Emotion overcame her and she breathed quickly, fighting back the tears. 'I . . . He . . . he said it was stifling in the lorry and he'd had to get a breath of fresh air on the Stowerton By-pass. He walked in the fields a bit where it was cool.'

'Think carefully, Mrs. Hatton. Did he say he had seen anything of interest while he was in those fields?'

She looked at him in bewilderment. 'No, he only said it had done him good. He felt fine, he said, and I could see he did. On top of the world he was that night, a different man. He was having his meal and we talked about Jack's wedding.' Her voice grew hoarse and she leant heavily against Jack's arm. 'Charlie wanted me to have a whole new outfit, dress, coat, hat, the lot. He said—he said I was his wife and he wanted me to be a credit to him.'

'And you always were, love. Charlie was proud of you.'

'What happened the next day?' said Wexford.

'We had a bit of a lay-in.' She bit her lip. 'Charlie got up at nine and then he phoned a fellow he knew who was leaving his flat. Charlie'd said he'd come down and look at it when he'd had his breakfast and that's what he did. You tell it, Jack, it's your turn.'

Jack eased away his arm and patted the widow's hand.

'Charlie came down to the works but I couldn't get away. I was off doing the wiring in them new houses over Pomfret way. He said he reckoned he'd found us a flat and I said, take Marilyn with you. I can see him now; old Charlie, pleased as punch and grinning like he always did when he was going to do something for you. Bobbing up and down he was like a monkey on a stick.' He sighed and shook his head. 'Old Charlie,' he said.

Impatiently, Wexford turned to the wife. 'You went with him?'

'Yeah, he came down to Moran's.' Moran's was Kingsmarkham's biggest draper's. 'That old bitch, that manageress, didn't want me to go at first. Not that there's much trade to speak of on a Monday morning. I'm leaving in a month anyway, I said, and if you don't like it you can give me my cards and I'll go now. Straight out I said it. I'd made her look real small in front of Charlie and she never said another word. Well, me and Charlie we went to look at this flat and there was this geezer who was leaving, a right queer if you ask me, wanted two hundred quid key money before he'd let us have it. I could have smacked his face then and there. In a dressing gown he was. There'll be forced labour for his sort one of these fine days and I was just going to come out with it when Charlie said that was all right and we'd find the money somehow. He could see I was dead keen on the place.'

'He paid over the money?'

'Don't be so daft. He said something about consulting with Jack, though if I wanted it Jack'd want it too all right, and then we went. I was fuming. I'll put up the money, Charlie said when we was outside, and you can pay me back when you're rolling. How about that, then?'

'Yes,' said Jack, 'how about that?'

'Did Hatton take you back to the shop?'

'Of course he didn't, he wasn't my keeper. He walked up with me as far as the Olive and then he said he'd got to make a phone call. He went into that box outside the Olive and I never saw him again for a couple of days.'

'Why would he make a phone call from a box when he had his own phone at home?'

The married pair were thinking what he, under other circumstances, might have thought. A married man with a phone of his own makes calls from a box to his mistress. Mrs. Hatton looked innocent, subdued, armoured by her memories. Then Marilyn laughed harshly. 'You're crazy if you're thinking what I think you are! Charlie Hatton?'

'What do you mean, Marilyn?' the widow asked.

'I'm thinking nothing,' said Wexford. 'Did your husband come home for his lunch?'

'About half-past twelve. I asked him what he was going to do with himself in the afternoon and it was then he said he was going to get his teeth seen to. He kept getting bits of food under his plate, you see. He was very ashamed of having false teeth was Charlie on account of being so young and all that. And on account of me . . . He thought I minded. Me mind? I wouldn't have cared if . . . Oh, what's the use? I was telling you about getting his teeth fixed. He'd often said he'd see about getting his teeth fixed. He'd often said he'd see about getting a real good set when he could afford it and he said he thought he'd go to Mr. Vigo.'

'I'd sort of recommended him, you see,' Jack put in.

'You?' Wexford said rudely.

Jack lifted his face and flushed a deep wine colour.

'I don't mean I went to him for my teeth,' he muttered. 'I'd been up at his place once or twice doing electrical work and I'd sort of described what the place was like to Charlie. Sort of about the garden and all the old things he's got up there and that room full of Chinese stuff.'

Mrs. Hatton was crying now and she wiped her eyes, smiling reminiscently through her tears. 'Many's the laugh Charlie and Jack used to have over that,' she said. 'Charlie said he'd like to see it. Like to have a dekko, he said, and Jack said Mr. Vigo was rolling in money. Well, he'd have to be a good dentist to make all that, wouldn't he? So Charlie thought he was the man for him and he phoned then and there. You'll never get an appointment for today, I said, but he did. Mr. Vigo had a cancellation and he said he'd see him at two.'

'And then?'

'Charlie came back at four and said Mr. Vigo was going to fix him up with a new set. Mr. Vigo was as nice as pie, he said, no side to him. He'd given him a drink in this said Chinese room and Charlie said when he was rich he was going to have stuff like that, rooms

full of it and vases and ornaments and—and a little
army of chess men and ... Oh God, he'll never have
anything where he is!'

'Don't, Lily, don't love.'

'When did Mr. Hatton give you the key money for
this flat of yours?'

'It was a loan,' said Marilyn Pertwee indignantly.

'Lend it to you, then?'

'He come round with it to Jack's dad's place on the
Wednesday.'

'That would have been the 22nd?'

'I reckon. We handed it over to this bloke as had the
flat the next day.' Jack Pertwee stared hard at Wexford.
The dull eyes were glazed now, the face pallid yet mottled. Wexford could hardly suppress a shiver. God help
the man who murdered Charlie Hatton, he thought, if
Pertwee gets on to him before we do.

'Isn't it about time we got shot of that thing?'

Sheila removed Clytemnestra from her father's chair
and contemplated the mass of hairs the dog had moulted
on to the cushion. 'I'm getting a bit fed up with her
myself,' she said. 'Sebastian's supposed to be coming
for her tonight.'

'Thank God for that.'

'All right if I have the car to take him to the station?'

'What, is he scared to cross those fields alone?' Mabel, dear, listen here, there's a robbery in the park ...
'I may want the car. He's young and healthy. Let
him walk.'

'He's got a verruca,' said Sheila. 'He had to walk
here and back when he brought her a fortnight ago. I'd
be meeting him now—' she gave her father a disgruntled look—'only you've always got the car.'

'It is my car,' said Wexford absurdly, and then, because it was a game that he and Sheila played, 'It was
my turquoise. I had it of Leah when I was a bachelor.
I would not have given it ...'

'For a wilderness of verrucas! Oh, Pop, you're a honey really. There's Sebastian now.'

Mrs. Wexford began calmly laying the table. 'Don't say anything about his hair,' she said to her husband. 'He's got peculiar hair and vou know what you are.'

Sebastian's hair resembled Clytemnestra's, only it wasn't grey. It hung on to his shoulders in shaggy curls.

'I hope the Swoofle Hound hasn't been too much of a bore for you, Mr. Wexford.'

Wexford opened his mouth to make some polite denial but Clytemnestra's transports at the sight of her owner made speech impossible for a while. She hurled herself at his long legs and plummeted her body against his jacket, a garment which Wexford incredulously identified as part of the full dress uniform of a commander in the Royal Norwegian Navy.

'You'll stay and have a meal?' said Mrs. Wexford.

'If it isn't too much trouble.'

'How was Switzerland?'

'All right. Expensive.' Wexford was beginning to nourish the unkind thought that the holdiay would have been even more costly had he had to pay boarding kennels fees, when Sebastian disarmed him by producing from his haversack a large box of chocolates for Mrs. Wexford.

'Suchard!' said Mrs. Wexford. 'How kind.'

Encouraged, Sebastian made short work of roast beef and Yorkshire pudding, occasionally reaching under the table to fondle Clytemnestra's ears.

'I'll drive you to the station,' said Sheila and she gave her father a confident smile.

'That'd be great. We might take Clytemnestra into that Olive place. She likes beer and it'd be a treat for her.'

'Not in my car, you don't,' said Wexford firmly.

'Oh, Pop!'

'Sorry, sweetheart. but you don't drink and drive.'

Sebastian's expression combined admiration for the daughter and a desire to ingratiate himself with the father. 'We'll walk down.' He shrugged. 'It's such a hell of a way to your station, though.' He eyed the banana custard. 'Yes, thanks, I will have some more. The trouble is I'll have to walk Sheila back, unless she goes home by the road,' he added unchivalrously. 'We heard about your murder even in Switzerland. Down in those fields at the back, wasn't it?'

Wexford seldom talked shop at home. Probably this young man wasn't pumping him and yet ... He gave a noncommital nod.

'Odd,' Sebastian said. 'I went to the station that way a fortnight ago, across the fields.'

Wexford intercepted his wife's glance, deflected it, said nothing. Sheila said it for him.

'What time was it, Seb? About ten?'

'A bit after that. I didn't meet a soul and I can't say I'm sorry.' He ruffled the dog's curly coat. 'If I hadn't jumped smartly out of the way, Clytemnestra, you mightn't ever have seen your papa again. Big American car nearly ran me down.'

'They do nip into that station approach,' said Sheila.

'Station approach, nothing. This was in the fields. In that lane that leads up to that stile thing. Great green car swept in at about forty and I practically had to dive into the hedge. I took the number actually but what with all the kerfuffle about the holiday I lost the bit of paper I wrote it on.'

'A courting couple?' said Wexford lightly.

'Could have been. I was too busy taking the number to look and I was scared of losing my train.'

'Well we won't go by the fields this time, and I'll trail all the way back by the road if it makes you happy, Pop.'

'You can take the car,' said Wexford. 'Stick to bitter lemon in the Olive, eh?'

17

'HERE'S MY THEORY,' said Burden, 'for what it's worth. I've been thinking about it, though, and it's the only possible solution. We've talked a lot about hired assassins but the only hired assassin in this case was Charlie Hatton, hired by Bridgit Culross's boy friend.'

'Fertile,' said Wexford, 'but I'd like it amplified.'

Burden shifted his chair a little nearer those of Wexford and the doctor. The wind and the sunlight filled the office with a pattern of dancing leaves. 'Jay is a rich man. He must be if he can afford to pay for three months in that clinic of yours just because his wife's having a difficult pregnancy.'

'Money down the drain,' commented Crocker. 'Do just as well on the N.H.S.'

'He's rich enough to pay someone to do his killing for him. You can bet your life he's a one-time friend of McCloy's. He arranges for Hatton to be waiting on that by-pass at the point where he's going to drop the girl on their way back from this conference.'

'Just what conference, Mike? Have we checked on Brighton conferences that weekend?'

'The National Union of Journalists, the Blake Society and the Gibbonites all met there,' said Burden promptly.

'What are the last lot?' put in the doctor, 'a bunch of monkeys?'

'Not gibbons,' said Burden, unsmiling. 'Gibbon. *The Decline and Fall* man. the historian. I reckon they're just another collection of cranks.'

'And Jay took a girl to Brighton, but left her alone

all day while he gossiped about Gibbon?' said Wexford thoughtfully. 'Well, stranger things have happened. Go on.'

'He faked a quarrel with her in the car on the way back to London and turfed her out of the car in a rage. Hatton was waiting for her, hit her over the head, emptied her handbag and made off back to his lorry. The next day Jay paid him his blood money. You can be sure that call Hatton made from a phone box was to Jay, telling him that the deed was done. And no one would have been any the wiser if Hatton hadn't been greedy and started soaking Jay.'

The doctor made a derisive face. 'Pardon me as mere layman, but that's a load of rubbish. I'm not saying the girl couldn't have been dead before the car hit her. She could have. But why should Hatton put her in the road? He couldn't be sure a car would come along and hit her. Besides, he could so easily have been seen. And he was a small man. He wouldn't have had the strength to carry her across the southbound highway. Why bother, anyway? If her death was supposed to look like the work of some vagrant maniac, why not kill her behind the hedge and leave her there?'

'What's your idea then?' said Burden sourly.

Crocker looked uppish. 'I don't have to have theories. I'm not paid for this kind of diagnosis.'

'Come down from your perch, Paracelsus,' said Wexford, 'and put yourselves in our shoes for a moment. Have a shot at it.'

'The trouble with you lot is you believe everything you're told. I don't. I know from experience people distort the truth because they're afraid or they have a psychological block or they want to be over-helpful. They leave things out because they're ignorant and when you tell them you want to know everything, they sort out what everything is to them. It's not necessarily everything to the expert who's asking the questions.'

'I know all that,' said Wexford impatiently.

'Then, Mrs. Fanshawe says the girl wasn't in the car, not because she's ashamed to admit it but because she's literally forgotten. Of course she was in the car. She hitched a lift a couple of miles before the crash and all that period is a blank to Mrs. Fanshawe. Naturally she's not trying to clear the blank. The very word "girl" is a red rag to a bull to her. You're bothered because there were no keys and no other identification in that expensive handbag. She left them in her suitcase and she left that suitcase in Jay's car.'

'Why?'

'So that Jay would have to come back for her. It was on the seat and after a few miles he'd realise and come back. Or so she thought. When he didn't she knew she could get it back all right at a later date. Presumably she knew where Jay lived. *In extremis* it would be an excuse for having it out with him and confronting the wife.'

'But Jay didn't come back and she got fed-up with waiting, so she hitched a lift from Fanshawe.'

'That's the simple natural solution, isn't it?'

'What you're saying amounts to that Jay is just a more or less harmless philanderer. Why didn't he come forward when we found the girl?'

The doctor gave a sardonic and superior laugh. 'Thanks to a spot of inefficiency on someone's part, you told the Press the dead girl was Nora Fanshawe. Why should Jay stick his neck out? If he'd ditched the girl on the outskirts of Stowerton it was because he never wanted to see her again. He's not likely to pop up and help you with your enquiries.'

Wexford said quietly, 'Where does Charlie Hatton come into all this?'

'If you don't mind, I'll answer that question with a question of my own. What makes you think he didn't have a source of supply completely separate from McCloy or Fanshawe or Jay?'

Wexford looked at Burden and he saw uneasiness creep into the inspector's face. He couldn't allow for this sort of doubt. It was unthinkable. 'He was behind that hedge,' he said stoutly. 'He saw that girl pushed into the road.'

'Get away!'

'Oh, not from the central strip of grass.' Wexford
paused for effect. The quivering leaf shadows played,
danced and died as the sun went in. 'From a car,' he
said, 'she was thrown out of a car.'

The sunlight came and went intermittently. Alone
now, Wexford watched the cloud masses drift above
the High Street roofs and cast their shadows now on a
house front, now on the road itself. The sun blazed
briefly, appearing from time to time embedded in a
golden nest.

Presently he took his railway timetable from his desk
drawer and looked up the afternoon trains to London.
There was a fast one at two-fifteen.

The lift was waiting for him, its door invitingly open.
By now Wexford had lost all his inhibitions about it.
He stepped inside and pressed the ground-floor button.
The door closed with a whisper and sank on a sigh.

Someone on the first floor must have summoned it,
for it trembled and its floor seemed to rise a fraction.
Then it shivered and stopped. Wexford waited for the
door to slide but nothing happened.

It was a solid door with neither glass nor grille. Impatiently Wexford tapped his foot. He glanced at the
control panel and wondered why the light marked one
hadn't come on. Probably it had been summoned and
whoever was waiting had got bored and used the stairs.
In that case, why wasn't the light on? He stuck his
thumb on the ground-floor button. Nothing happened.

Or rather, the worst, what he had always feared, had
happened. The damned thing had broken. It had got
stuck. Very likely it was between floors. A tremor of
panic touched one corner of his brain and he dismissed
it with a fierce oath. He tapped smartly on the door.

Was the thing sound-proof? Wexford had never had
much faith in soundproofing methods, having lived
during the early part of his career in a series of flats
highly commended by their agents for the seaweed
board allegedly incorporated in their walls and ceilings.

They hadn't stopped him being driven nearly mad by the piano from upstairs and the incessant drumming of children's feet. They couldn't sound-proof a dwelling house, he thought furiously. It would be just like 'them' to succeed in the utterly pointless achievement of sound-proofing a lift. He knocked on the door again and then he pressed the button marked Emergency. If anything, the little black and gilt box settled into an even deeper immobility.

There was a little leather seat, like the extra seats in a taxi, folded into the wall. Wexford pulled it down. It creaked when he sat on it. Glancing about him with simulated ease, he assessed the volume of the lift. Seven by four by four. As far as he could see there was no means of letting air in or carbon dioxide out. He listened. He might have been stone deaf, the silence was so deep.

How long could anybody as big as he remain confined in a space seven by four by four? He had no idea. It was ten minutes to two. He got up and the seat snapped back into the wall. The sound made him jump. He brought both fists down against the panelling and pounded hard. The lift quivered and that disquieted him. For all he knew it was hanging by a thread.

It might be better to shout. But shout what? 'Help, let me out!' was too humiliating to consider.

'Is there anyone there?' he called, and because that sounded like a medium in a sèance, 'Hey, the lift's stuck!'

Under the circumstances, it would be wiser to save his breath. It was possible that most of the rooms were empty. Burden and Martin and Loring were all out. Camb might be sitting downstairs (downstairs!) at his desk. Someone would be sitting there. It was equally certain that his cries were unheard.

With an unpleasant sinking feeling, Wexford faced the fact that unless Burden returned two hours earlier than he had said, it was likely that no one would want to use the lift. Camb was at his post, Martin in Sewingbury. It hadn't escaped Wexford's notice that most of the uniformed branch preferred the stairs. He might be there till tea-time and if so, would he still be alive at tea-time?

Two o'clock. If he didn't get out in five minutes he would miss that train. That didn't matter too much. Without checking at the Princess Louise Clinic, he was almost sure he had the answer. Guesswork perhaps, but inspired guesswork. If he died they would never know . . .

Sick of shouting, he flapped down the seat again. Probably it was only his fancy that the air in the tiny box was growing thick. Panic would not help at all. It was outside the indulgences he allowed himself. Outside them too was the thread of terror that told him he was a rat in a hole, a fox in a stopped earth. Briefly he thought of Sheila. No more of that, that way madness lies . . .

Two-fifteen, Wexford took out his notebook and a pencil. At any rate, he could write it all down.

'I don't know where he gets his crazy ideas,' said the doctor indiscreetly. Burden gave him a neutral smile. 'If I was in your place I'd want to try it out. Have you got something else on this afternoon?'

'Nothing Martin and Loring can't see to without me.'

'Shall we take my car, then?'

'Don't you have a surgery?' asked Burden, who thought the whole plan unorthodox.

'My afternoon off. I rather like this dabbling in forensics.'

Burden didn't. He wondered what Crocker would say if he suggested accompanying him to a patient's bedside. 'All right,' he said reluctantly. 'But not the by-pass, for heaven's sake.'

'Cheriton airfield,' said the doctor.

The place hadn't been used for years. It lay on the far side of Cheriton forest beyond Pomfret and it was a favourite haunt of L-drivers. Teenagers below the permitted age of provisional licence holders got their parents to bring them on to the disused runways where they kangaroo-hopped in comparative safety.

Today it was deserted. The greens between the runways had been ploughed up and used for a turnip and sugar beet crop. Beyond the rows of regularly planted beet the pine forest climbed over gently undulating hills.

'You can drive,' said the doctor. I fancy the victim's role.'

'Rather you than I,' said Burden, who was wearing his new Gannex.

He shifted into the driving seat. The runway was as broad as the northbound highway of the Stowerton Bypass.

'Presumably she was a strong healthy girl,' said Crocker. 'You couldn't push anyone like that out of a moving vehicle if she was in full possession of her faculties. He must have hit her on the head first.'

'You're suggesting he had an unconscious girl beside him?'

'They'd had a row and he'd socked her,' said the doctor laconically. 'Now I'm her and I'm unconscious. The road is clear. You wouldn't do it from the fast lane, though, would you? Something might just come whizzing up behind you and that'd be awkward. So it's the middle lane. Go on, move over.'

Burden eased into the centre of the runway. 'That row of beet on the right corresponds to the central strip,' he said. 'Fanshawe swerved to the right to avoid the body.'

'So *he* says.'

'What do I do? Leave the passenger door on the latch?'

'I reckon so. Trickle along and then push me out.'

Crocker rolled himself into a ball, his arms around his knees. Burden didn't dare drive at more than a snail's pace. He was doing five miles an hour. He leaned across, swung the door wide and gave the doctor a light push. Crocker rolled easily into the road, staggered and stood up. Burden stopped.

'You see?' Crocker dusted himself off with a grimace. 'I told you he was crazy. See where I landed? Right in the slow lane. And you'd hardly got the car moving. Our mystery man was going at a fair lick. The girl would have rolled right over to the left, almost on to the grass verge.'

'D'you want to try it in the fast lane, just for the record?'

'Once is enough,' said the doctor firmly. 'You can see what would happen, anyway. The girl mightn't have rolled into the slow lane, but she'd have landed in the *middle of the road*. You just couldn't get a body into the fast lane itself from a moving car.'

'You're right. Necessarily, having been thrown from the left, it would roll towards the left, in which case Fanshawe in the fast lane would have passed cleanly to the right of it.'

'Or if mystery man was in fact driving in the fast lane and the body landed plumb in that lane, Fanshawe would have swerved to the *left* to avoid it and never hit that tree in the central strip. There's only one possibility and we've proved that's not tenable.'

Burden was sick of being told his job. 'Exactly,' he said hastily. 'If the girl was thrown out to the right and her head was towards the middle lane with her feet towards the central strip, only then might Fanshawe have swerved to the right. He would have swerved instinctively to avoid the head.'

'But that, as we know, is impossible. If you're driving a car you can only throw someone out from the passenger seat on the left, not from one of the back seats, and that means the victim is always going to land way over to the left.'

'I'll go back and tell him,' said Burden thoughtfully, and he let the doctor take the wheel to drive them back along the runway between the lines of green leaves.

'Chief Inspector gone out?' Coming out of Wexford's office, Burden encountered Loring in the corridor.

'I don't know, sir. Isn't he in his office?'

'You imagine he's hiding under his desk, do you, or maybe he's filed himself away in the filing cabinet.'

'I'm sorry, sir.' Loring raised a yellow venetian blind. 'His car's there.'

'I know that.' Burden had come up by the stairs. He went towards the lift, pressed the button to summon it. When he had waited a minute and it hadn't come, he shrugged and walked down to the ground floor. Sergeant Camb turned from the woman who had lost a Siamese cat.

'Mr. Wexford? He hasn't gone out.'

'Then where the hell is he?' Burden never swore, even as mildly as that. Camb stared. 'He was going to London. I'd reckoned he'd go on the two-fifteen.'

It was half-past three. 'Maybe he went out the back way.'

'Why should he? He never does unless he's going into court.'

'Blue eyes,' said the woman plaintively, 'and a coffee coloured mark on his neck.'

The sergeant sighed. 'All Siamese cats have blue eyes and brown marks on their backs, madam.' He picked up his pen and said to Burden, 'To tell you the truth, I've been tied up all the afternoon, trying to get hold of the engineers to see to that lift. Inspector Letts said it wouldn't come when he pressed the button. I reckon it's stuck between floors.'

'And I reckon,' said Burden, 'Mr. Wexford is stuck in it.'

'My God, you don't mean it, sir?'

'Give me that phone. D'you realise he's been in there nearly two hours? *Give me that phone.*'

It was afternoon visiting at Stowerton Infirmary. It was also consultant's day. That meant an exodus of hundreds of cars which the woman on traffic patrol usually controlled efficiently. Today, however, a huge bluish-green car with battered fins, parked half across the drive, blocked the exit. It was locked, keyless, immovable, and behind it a traffic jam stretched nose to tail from the car park.

In vain four ambulance men had tried to lift it and hump it against the gate of the porter's lodge. Presently Vigo, the orthodentist, got out of his own car to lend a hand. He was bigger and more powerful than any of the ambulance men, but all their combined efforts couldn't shift it.

'Probably belongs to someone visiting a private patient,' said Vigo to the consultant gynaecologist whose car had come to a standstill behind his.

'Better get a porter to ring the private wing.'

'And fast,' said Vigo. 'These people ought to be shot. I've got an appointment at four.'

And it was five to when Nurse Rose knocked on Mrs. Fanshawe's door. 'Excuse me, Mr. Jameson, but your car's blocking the drive. Could you move it please? It's not just visitors that want to get out.' Her voice took on an awed tone. Outrage had been committed. 'Personal request of Mr. Vigo and Mr. Delauney. So if you wouldn't mind . . .'

Michael Jameson got up languidly. 'I don't know these guys.' He gave Nurse Rose a long appraising look. 'But I wouldn't want you to get in bad with them, sweetheart. I'll shift it.'

Nora Fanshawe touched his sleeve. 'You'll come back for me, Michael?'

'Sure, don't fuss.' Nurse Rose opened the door for him and he walked out ahead of her. 'Dead bore, this hospital visiting,' the women in the room heard him say.

Mrs. Fanshawe had painted her face for the first time since regaining consciousness. Now she touched up her thin lips with scarlet and rubbed at the eyeshadow which had settled in greasy streaks into the folds of her lids. 'Well?' she said.

'Well what, Mother?'

'I take it you're going to marry that waster?'

'I am and you'll have to get used to it.'

'Your father would never have allowed it if he were alive,' said Mrs. Fanshawe, twisting her rings.

'If my father were alive, Michael wouldn't want to marry me. I wouldn't have any money you see. I'm being quite frank with you. I thought that's what parents wanted, frankness from their children.' She shrugged and flicked a fair hair from the shoulder of her blue suit. Her voice was ugly, stripped bald of convention and pretence. 'I wrote to him and told him my father was dead.' She laughed. 'He came down here like a shot. I've bought him,' she said. 'I tried the product and liked it and now I'm going to keep it. The principle is that of the mail order catalogue.'

Mrs. Fanshawe wasn't shocked. She hadn't taken her eyes from her daughter's face and she hadn't flinched. 'All right,' she said. 'I can't stop you. I won't quarrel with you, Nora.' Her voice didn't quaver. 'You're all I've got, all I've ever had.'

'Then is there no reason why we shouldn't be a happy little family. is there?'

'A happy family! Frank you may be, but you're deceiving yourself. He's got his eye on that nurse already.'

'I know.'

'And you think you've bought him!' All Mrs. Fanshawe's self-control couldn't stop the bitterness breaking through. 'Buying people! You know where you get it from, don't you? Your father. You're your father all over again, Nora. God knows, I tried to keep you innocent, but he taught you, he taught you people could be bought.'

'Oh, no, Mother,' said Nora Fanshawe equably. 'You taught me. Shall we have some more tea?' And she rang the bell.

At four-fifteen the lift slid down to the ground floor. The door began to slide and Burden felt sick, his bowels turned to water. He couldn't look. The two engineers came down the stairs, running.

The foyer was full of people. Grinswold, the Chief

Constable, Inspector Lewis and Letts, Martin, Loring, Camb and, nearest the lift, Dr. Crocker.

The door was open. Burden had to look. He stepped forward, pushing people aside.

'Gangway!' said the doctor.

'Wexford came out, grey in the face, the doctor's arm about his shoulders. He took two heavy steps.

'Bricked up,' he said, 'like a bloody nun!'

'God, sir. Are you all right?'

'It's all in the book,' Wexford gasped. 'I've got it all down in the book. Nothing . . .' he said, 'nothing like a rarefied atmosphere for making the brain work. Cheaper than going up Everest, that lift.'

And then he collapsed into the sling Crocker and Letts made with their arms.

'I'm just going off duty,' said Nurse Rose, 'and the night staff are in the kitchen, so you won't mind finding your own way, will you?' She peered at him in the dim light of the corridor. 'Didn't you come visiting Mrs. Fanshawe? I thought so. You'll know where to go, then. He's in room five, next door but one to hers.'

Burden thanked her. Turning the corner, he came face to face with Mrs. Wexford and Sheila.

'How is he?'

'He's fine. No after-effects. They're only keeping him in for the night to be on the safe side.'

'Thank God!'

'You really care about poor old Pop, don't you?' When she smiled, he could have kissed her, she looked so like her father. Crazy, really, that this enchanting perfect face was the copy and the essence of the heavy wrinkled face that had been haunting him all the time he had made out his arrest and read out the charge. He didn't want to seem sentimental and he managed a cheerful grin. 'He's dying to see you,' she said. 'We were just a stop-gap.'

Wexford lay in bed in a room that was just like Mrs. Fanshawe's. He had an old red checked dressing gown around his shoulders and a fuzz of grey hair showed between the lapels of his pyjama jacket. A grin curled the corners of his mouth and his eyes snapped.

Tip-toeing, Burden crossed to the bed. Everyone in hospital tip-toes, except the staff, so he did too, glancing nervously about him. The cooking smell and the disinfectant smell with which the corridor was redolent were drowned in here by the carnations Mrs. Wexford had brought her husband.

'How are you feeling?'

'Perfectly all right, of course,' Wexford said impatiently. 'All those damned flowers. Makes the place look like a chapel of rest. I'd come out now only that bloody Crocker and his henchmen keep getting at me, sapping my strength.' He sat up with a jerk and scowled. 'Open that beer, will you? Sheila brought those cans in for me. She's a good girl, chip off the old block.'

Burden rinsed the glass from Wexford's supper tray and from the washbasin took the toothglass for himself. 'A private room, eh? Very grand.'

Wexford chuckled. 'Not my idea, Mike. They were heading for the general ward when Crocker remembered Monkey Matthews was in, having his veins done. We came to the conclusion it might be an embarrassment to him after I did him a couple of years ago for stealing by finding. Don't worry, I'll take care to tell him what saving his face has cost me.' He looked round him complacently. 'Eight quid a day, this room. Good thing I wasn't in that lift any longer.' He drank his beer, wiped his mouth with a man-size Kleenex. 'Well, have you done the deed?'

'At five-thirty.'

'Pity I wasn't there.' Suddenly he shivered. 'The skin of my teeth ...' Then he laughed. 'Teeth!' he said. 'That's funny.'

Footsteps that didn't tiptoe sounded outside and Crocker marched in. 'Who gave you leave to have a booze-up?'

'Sit down, not on the bed. Nurse Rose doesn't like it. We were just going to have a post-mortem. Interested?'

The doctor fetched himself a chair from the empty

room next door. He flopped into it. 'I've heard who it is over the grapevine. By God, you could have knocked me down with a feather.'

'I leave that to others,' said Wexford. 'The intemperate fellows who aren't content with feathers. They use stones.' He met the doctor's eyes and saw there the astonishment and the eagerness for enlightenment he loved to see. 'Murderers aren't unknown among the medical profession,' he said. 'What about Crippen? Buck Ruxton? This time it happened to be a dentist.'

18

'IT'S ALWAYS A problem,' said Wexford, 'to know where to begin. Where's the beginning? I often think novelists must have my trouble. Well, I know they do. I used to know a chap who wrote books. He said it was easy to end and the middle just happened naturally, but he never knew where to begin. How far do you have to go back in a man's life to find what makes him do things? To his childhood, to his parents, to Adam?'

'Let's not go back that far,' said Burden. 'We'll be here all night.'

Wexford grinned at him. He banged his pillows and pulled their corners round his shoulders. 'I think I'll begin ten years ago,' he said. 'But don't worry. You know how time flies.'

'Vigo wasn't here ten years ago.'

'He was getting married. He married a rich girl, probably not entirely for her money. But the money set him up in practice here and bought his house for him. They had a child.'

'It was mongoloid,' said the doctor. 'Been in an institution since it was six months old. Vigo took it very hard.'

'Who wouldn't?' said Wexford. 'Look at Vigo. What Hitler would have called the perfect Aryan type and clever with it. If you were stud farming humans, wouldn't you choose Vigo as your ideal stallion?' The doctor gave a grudging nod.

'And if you were Vigo, wouldn't you expect to sire splendid progeny?"

'Everyone does.'

'Maybe. Everyone hopes, let's say, and sometimes the most unexpected people are lucky.' He smiled to himself and finished the last drop of beer Sheila had brought. 'I reckon Vigo blamed his wife. Don't tell me that was unfair. Life's unfair. They didn't have any more children for eight years.'

The doctor leant forward. 'They've got a son now,' he sighed. 'Poor kid.'

'If he's poor it's his father's fault,' Wexford snapped. 'Don't give me that sentimental stuff. This is the real beginning, Mrs. Vigo's second pregnancy. She had high blood pressure, she got toxaemia.'

'A threatened toxaemia, surely,' the doctor corrected him pedantically.

'Whatever it was, she was admitted to the Princess Louise Clinic in New Cavendish Street two months before the birth. You can imagine Vigo's feelings, was it going to go wrong again?'

'Toxaemia doesn't lead to mongoloid babies.'

'Oh, shut up!' said Wexford irritably. 'People don't reason in cases like that. He was scared and depressed and he took up with one of the nurses he met when he was visiting his wife. Maybe he'd always been a bit of a philanderer. I've got my own reasons for thinking that.'

'In your notes,' said Burden, who had the book open on his lap, 'you said he dropped Bridget Culross after the child was born healthy and normal.'

'That's conjecture. Let's say he was too taken up with the child—he's crazy about that child—to bother about outside interests. Did you check with the clinic?'

'I did. Mrs. Vigo was admitted last October and remained in the clinic until two weeks after the child was born at the end of December. Bridget Culross was on duty in the ward where her room was from November 1st until January 1st.'

Wexford leaned back. 'It had to be someone with a Christian or surname beginning with J, you see. Jerome Fanshawe, we thought at first, but that couldn't be because Mrs. Fanshawe was past the age of childbearing. I seriously considered Michael Jameson. It wouldn't at all surprise me to know he's got a wife somewhere.' He lowered his voice. Mrs. Fanshawe was two doors down the corridor. 'A Michael Jameson might just as well call himself Jay as Mike and he had the right kind of car. But we'll come to that later. Anyway, it wasn't either of them. It was Jolyon Vigo. With a name like that you'd be glad of a convenient abbreviation sometimes.'

'You say he dropped the girl. Why did he take up with her again?'

'A man has a child,' said Wexford. 'If he worships the child it may, for a while, bring him closer to his wife. But these things wear off. Can the leopard change his spots? The girl thought she'd a chance of getting him to marry her. No doubt, he'd even considered that when he thought his wife wasn't ever going to give him a child. Now he wanted his bit of fun on the side but he wasn't going to lose his son for it. Not on your life. And that's the crux.'

The doctor crossed his legs and shifted his chair a little. 'Where does Charlie Hatton come into all this?'

Wexford didn't answer him directly. Instead he said, 'Vigo and Culross were carrying on their affair intermittently. If it wasn't all that of a regular thing, that's probably because the girl nagged him about marriage and he stalled.'

'You can't possibly know that,' Burden objected.

Wexford said loftily, 'I understand human nature. On the 18th of May Bridget Culross had a long weekend off and, by chance, the Blake Society were also having their weekend conference in Brighton over the next three days. Vigo picked Culross up at Marble Arch and drove her to Brighton in his car, a big Plymouth sedan.'

'How do you know it was the Blake Society? Why not the Gibbonites?'

'Vigo's got Blake drawings all over his hall walls. Did you check their room bookings?'

'They booked in at the Majestic in their own names. Two adjoining rooms. They vacated them on Monday afternoon, Monday May 20th.'

Wexford nodded. 'Perhaps it was their first weekend together. Bridget Culross spent it pressuring Vigo into agreeing to divorce his wife. Or trying to. I don't know what happened. How could I? I'll make a guess that she knew they'd have to pass through Kingsmarkham, or near it, on their way back to London, and she tried to persuade Vigo to take her back with him to the house in Ploughman's Lane and confront his wife together.' He cleared his throat. 'Men don't like that kind of thing,' he said. 'They had a fight. Want to know where? I guess she put the pressure on really hard when they reached the point where the road passes nearest to Kingsmarkham. That's about three miles south of the spot where the body was found. No doubt they got out of the car and my guess is the girl said she'd make her way to Ploughman's Lane on her own if he wouldn't come with her. Vigo's a big powerful man. They struggled, she fell and hit her head. He had an unconscious, perhaps dead, girl on his hands. You see his dilemma?'

'Whatever he did next, his wife would find out, divorce him and get custody of the child,' said Burden.

'Exactly. He began some quick thinking. First remove all identification from the expensive handbag he had given her himself. No doubt, a good many people knew where she had gone, but she had assured him no one knew his name. Vigo's an intelligent man, a medical man who knows something about police methods. They wouldn't search for a girl with a reputation like

Bridget Culross's and no near relatives to give a damn. Suppose she was found dead in the road, knocked down by a passing vehicle? It would be assumed she'd quarrelled with her boy-friend, hitched a lift to Stowerton and been knocked down crossing the road or trying to hitch a second lift. He put her on the passenger seat, laying her flat with her head on his lap so as not to mark the seat with blood. Probably he had a newspaper or an old rug to cover his knees, something he could burn when he got home.

'He entered the by-pass where at that time of night and during the week, the road was comparatively clear. Now he wouldn't dare drive too fast—no one could open a car door and throw a body out at any speed— so he kept to the slow lane.'

'What then?'

'Things went according to plan. He drove along at twenty or thirty miles an hour and when there were no other vehicles in sight, he shot the girl out and she landed as he had expected with her head well over into the fast lane . . .'

'Wait a minute,' said the doctor sharply. 'That's not possible. It can't be done. We tried it and . . .'

'Wait a minute by all means,' said Wexford, and in execrable French, *'Pas devant les infirmières.'*

'Tea, coffee, Ovaltine or Horlicks,' said a bright voice whose owner had tapped on the glass panel in the door.

'Ovaltine would be very wholesome,' said Wexford blandly. 'Thank you kindly.'

'A chiel's among ye, taking notes,' said Wexford. 'In other words, Charlie Hatton.' He sipped his Ovaltine with an inscrutable expression. 'He had parked his lorry in the lay-by just over the brow of the hill and was taking the air in the field on the other side of the hedge.'

'You mean he saw Vigo push a girl out of his car and did nothing about it?'

'Depends by what you mean by nothing. In my experience the Charlie Hattons of this world aren't over-anxious to get involved with the police even as indignant observers. Hatton did something. He blackmailed Vigo.'

'Can I have a couple of your grapes?' said the doctor. 'Thanks. The only grapes I ever taste are the ones I nick from my patients.' He put one in his mouth and chewed it, seeds and all. 'Did he know Vigo?'

'By sight, I daresay, or else he knew the car. You'll get appendicitis.'

'Rubbish, old wives' tale. Anyhow, I've had it. What happened next?'

Wexford took another Kleenex and wiped his mouth.

'Hatton went home to his wife. Five minutes later Jerome Fanshawe came along, driving like the clappers, spotted the girl in the road too late and shouted out, "My God!" She was lying, remember, with her body and legs in the middle lane and her head over the fast lane. Fanshawe swerved. Wouldn't it be instinctive in those circumstances to avoid the head at all costs? So he swerved to the *right,* mounted the turfed centre section and crashed into a tree. That, I think, sums up the entire intervention of the Fanshawes into this case. For once in his life, Fanshawe was the innocent victim.'

Burden nodded agreement and took up the tale. 'On the following morning,' he said, 'Hatton mulled over the whole business. He made his telephone call about the flat for Pertwee and then went down to see it with the girl Marilyn. Immediately there was a call on his purse. The tenant of the flat wanted two hundred pounds key money.'

'And that clinched it,' said Wexford. 'He left Marilyn at the Olive and Dove and she saw him go into a phone box. We may be sure he was phoning Vigo, making an appointment for the afternoon.'

'I thought you said he made the appointment later from his own home?' said the doctor.

'He *phoned* again from his home. That was just a blind for his wife. You may be sure he'd already made it clear to Vigo what he wanted and that he would phone again as if legitimately asking for an appointment. Of course it happened that way. If it hadn't, do you suppose Vigo would have agreed to an appointment that same day, only an hour afterwards? He's a busy man, booked up weeks in advance. Charlie Hatton wasn't even a patient of his. I've no doubt that in the morning Charlie told him he wanted hush money out of him and he'd have the best set of false teeth Vigo could provide. Free of charge, of course.'

'It must have been a hell of a shock to Vigo,' said Crocker thoughtfully. 'The night before he'd taken a risk and acted on the spur of the moment. The chances then of its coming out were fairly high, I'd have thought. But Fanshawe's crash was an unforeseen stroke of luck for him. Seeing it in the morning paper and seeing that the girl had been identified as Nora Fanshawe made him safe. By the time the real Nora turned up things would be so confused, the truth would very likely never come out. Who would have imagined his actions had been seen?'

'Naturally he paid up,' said Wexford. 'Paid and paid. My guess is that when he phoned the first time Hatton asked him to draw a thousand pounds immediately from his bank, a sum which he was to give to Hatton, and did give him, during his visit to Ploughman's Lane that afternoon, the afternoon of May 21st. Must have been rather bizarre, mustn't it, that consultation of Haton's? The mind boggles, as they say. You have to picture the blackmailer lying back in his chair with his mouth open while his victim, desperate, at bay, if you like, probed about, measuring him for his new teeth.'

'On the following day, May 22nd, we know Hatton paid five hundred pounds into his own account, keeping two hundred for the Pertwee's key money and the remaining three hundred for incidental expenses, furniture, clothes and other frivolity. The weekly payments of fifty pounds a time followed at once. I reckon Hatton got Vigo to leave the money in some prearranged hiding place down by the river on Friday nights somewhere along the route Hatton took on his way home from the darts club. And one Friday night . . .'

'Yes, why that particular Friday?'

'Who can say at what point the victim of blackmail reaches the end of his tether?'

'Mrs. Fanshawe,' put in Burden unexpectedly. 'You see, that wasn't quite right, what you said about the Fanshawes' intervention having come to an end. Mrs. Fanshawe regained consciousness the day before Hatton was killed. It was in the morning papers, just a paragraph, but it was there.'

'You've got something there, Mike. Nora was still missing, but once Mrs. Fanshawe could talk, Vigo might believe she'd tell us the girl's body couldn't be that of her daughter. Hatton was an important witness with someone else now to back up his story. Once he'd had all he wanted out of Vigo . . .'

The doctor got up, stood for a moment staring at Wexford's flowers and then said, 'It's a good story, but it's impossible. It couldn't have happened that way.' Wexford smiled at him. Crocker said irritably, 'What are you grinning like that for? I tell you there's an obvious flaw. If anyone throws a body out of a car, even feet first, it's going to fall well over to the left. Vigo would have had to be driving right on the grass section itself for the girl's head to have been in the fast lane. And as to that theory of yours about the head being on his lap to stop bloodstains getting on the passenger seat, it's nonsense. That way her *feet* would have been in the fast lane and Fanshawe would have swerved to the *left* to avoid her head.'

He stopped and gave a defiant snort as the nurse came back with a sleeping pill.

'I don't want that,' said Wexford. He slid down in the bed and pulled up the covers. 'I'll sleep, I'm tired.' Over the top of the sheet he said, 'Nice of you two to come. Oh, and by the way, it's a foreign car. Left-hand drive. Good night.'

19

'ELECTRICIAN,' SAID JACK Pertwee on the doorstep. 'You've got a switch that wants fixing.'

'Not me,' said the girl. 'I only work here. Wait a bit ... Is this it?' She fumbled among some loose sheets of paper on a table beneath the mullioned window and her face reddened with indignation. 'You was supposed to come last week."

'I was off last week. This is my first day back. Don't work yourself up. I've been here before. I can find my own way.'

His first day back. His first job on his first day, the first return to normal routine after the earthquake. Jack didn't know why he had chosen to come here—there were a dozen names who needed him on his list. Perhaps it was because some unformed unrecognised hunger in his subconscious cried for the solace and the refreshment of looking on beautiful things; perhaps because this place was unique in his experience, alien and remote from anywhere he had ever been with Charlie.

But as always when he found himself at the house in Ploughman's Lane, a clumsiness dragged at his feet and his deft fingers began to feel all thumbs. He was like a barbarian who, having entered a forsaken Roman villa, stood dazzled and amazed, overcome by the awe of ignorance. He crossed the hall and pretending to himself that he did not know the precise location of the switch—there was no need to, he was alone now—he opened door after door to peer in wonderment at the treasures within. A muttered 'Pardon me, lady' would have been his defence if one of them had been occu-

pied but there was no one about and Jack looked his
fill undisturbed at velvet and silk, dark tables inlaid
with ivory, pictures in gilt frames, flowered china holding real flowers, a bust in bronze, a pomander whose
orange spicy scent was brought to him on warm sunlight.

Afterwards he was unable to say what had suddenly
brought Charlie so vividly to his mind, except perhaps
that the memory of his dead friend was never far from
it. Maybe this flash of pain, sharper and more real than
any he had yet felt, came when he opened the door of
the Chinese room. It was here, just inside the door, that
his task awaited him and he stepped for a moment on
the threshold stunned into immobility by the strange
rich colours. It was too early yet for the sun to have
reached the back of the house but the reds and golds,
the unearthly sea greens and citrus yellows, blazed
fiercely enough in shadow. Jack put down his tool bag
and gazed about him numbly. He had been here before and yet it seemed to him that he had never seen
the room until this moment. It was as if his nerves had
been stripped raw and, unprotected, received the im-
pact of these glorious yet intolerable colours in a series
of vibrations like electric shocks.

Half in a trance he approached the chessmen that
Charlie had called an army and saw in the face of one
of them, a red knight, the perfect facsimile of his dead
friend's face, sharp, cunning, astute and kind. A long-
ing to possess and preserve it seized him but he was
afraid even to touch the delicate carved jade and he
heard himself give a low sob.

It was his awed and perhaps childlike descriptions of
this house which had, he supposed, led Charlie here.
Just as he, Jack, might have gone to the grocer's, so
Charlie Hatton had come here to buy the best. Jack's
sorrow dissolved in admiration of that audacity. His
friend had penetrated this museum too and that not as
a servant or a workman but as a customer. Vigo had
brought him into this room and drunk with him. Jack
could imagine Charlie's cocky poise, his hard brown

hands even daring to lift a cup or finger a silk picture
while he commented on its quality, its desirability, with
brash impudence. Had he recognised himself at the
head of that scarlet army? And the Philistines slew
Jonathan. . . . How are the mighty fallen and the weapons of war perished!

Jack turned away from the sharp little faces that
seemed to scrutinise him and, opening his bag, squatted
down in front of it. He felt worn out, exhausted at ten
in the morning, and the girl's voice behind him made
him jump.

'Thought you might fancy a cup of tea.'

He could guess his own expression and he didn't
want her to see his face. 'Mr. or Mrs. about?' he asked.
'I'd better see one of them.'

'Haven't you heard then? She's gone away and taken
the boy. The police arrested him yesterday for killing
that lorry driver.'

There had been tears in Jack's eyes and now his eyelids burned as they sometimes did after an evening with
Charlie in the smoke-filled bar of the Dragon. He was
staring into the heap of tools but not seeing them. His
brain had become an empty red space. He got to his
feet and there was a hammer in his hand, although he
couldn't remember selecting it from the heap.

The red light before his eyes split into a spectrum of
insane red and gold and sea green that roared as it
twisted and leapt about him, as if a kaleidoscope could
make sound as varied and as fantastic as its changing
pictures. Behind him another, shriller noise echoed.
The girl had begun to scream.

'A bull in a china shop,' said Wexford.

He picked his way through the fragments which lit-
tered the carpet, stopping occasionally to lift between
finger and thumb a sliver of transparent porcelain. His
expression was impassive and cold but a little heat entered it as he approached the table where the chessmen
had been. Not a piece remained intact, but here and
there among the red and white gravel he found a deli-

cate spear with an amputated hand still grasping it, a fragment of ivory lace, a horse's hoof.

Burden was kneeling down, smoothing out torn remnants of the silk pictures. A big rough footprint scarred the scales of the painted fish, the print of the same foot that had ground saké cups to dust.

'Frightening, isn't it?' said Wexford. 'Barbarity is frightening. I'm glad I don't know . . .'

'What all this stuff was worth?' Burden hazarded.

'Not so much as all that. I meant I'm glad I don't know it's uniqueness, its age, its quality really; looting must be like this, I suppose, wanton, revengeful.'

'You said Charlie Hatton was a soldier of fortune.'

'Yes. Is there any point in going to talk to his comrade-in-arms? I suppose we have to.'

Jack Pertwee was in the kitchen with Sergeant Martin. He was sitting down, his arms spread and his body slumped across the table. Wexford shook him roughly and jerked his head back. Their eyes met and for a moment Wexford still held on to the the electrician's coat collar, shaking it as might a man who has brought a destructive dog under control. Jack's jowls shook and his teeth chattered.

'You're a fool, Pertwee,' Wexford said scornfully. 'You'll lose your job over this. And for what? For a friend who's dead and can't thank you?'

His voice almost inaudible, Jack said, 'The best . . . The best friend a man ever had. And it was me sent him here.' He clenched his fist, drove it hard against the table.

'Oh, take him away, Sergeant.'

Jack dragged himself to his feet. His fist opened and something fell to the floor, rolled and came to rest at Wexford's feet. The chief inspector stared downwards. It was the red knight's decapitated head. The wicked sharp face, tricked into expression by a ribbon of sunlight, grinned widely and showed its teeth.

'Charlie,' Jack whispered. He tried to say it again but great agonised sobs tore away the name.

11